The Thirsty Land

Also by Norman A. Fox
in Thorndike Large Print

The Badlands Beyond
The Rawhide Years
Reckoning at Rimbow
Tall Man Riding

This Large Print Book carries the
Seal of Approval of N.A.V.H.

The
Thirsty Land

NORMAN A. FOX

Thorndike Press • Thorndike, Maine

Library of Congress Cataloging in Publication Data:

Fox, Norman A., 1911-1960.
    The thirsty land / Norman A. Fox.
        p. cm.
    ISBN 1-56054-347-7 (alk. paper : lg. print)
    1. Large type books. I. Title.
[PS3511.O968T45   1992]   91-44756
813'.54—dc20   CIP

This novel is a work of fiction. Names, characters, places and incidents are either the product of the author's imagination or are used fictitiously. Any resemblance to actual events or locales or persons, living or dead, is entirely coincidental.

Thorndike Press Large Print edition published in 1992 by arrangement with Richard C. Fox.

Cover design by Harry Swanson.

The tree indicium is a trademark of Thorndike Press.

This book is printed on acid-free, high opacity paper. ∞

The Thirsty Land

1

Return to the Range

He had remembered this land with longing through the thousand days since he'd last looked upon it. He had hungered for flatness and tawny desolation and unending emptiness and the tang of sage, sometimes recalling these things as a dream is recalled. Across these last miles he had craned his neck often from the day coach's window, seeing the prairie's lean and hungry look, seeing the burned-out dryness of it, and wondering how the reality could differ so greatly from the dream. Wayne had written of the drought, of course, and so had Cynthia. But even the high ramparts of the Rimfires were changed; they had no snow upon their peaks; and he could remember no time when the mountains had looked so bald. Such cattle as he'd seen from the train had been spiritless beasts, scrawny and dejected; and he had shaken his head at the sight of them, wondering what had come over the land and feeling cheated because his homecoming was not as he'd imagined it.

When he climbed down from the coach at Ballardton, he paused for a moment on the last step and had his look at the town, and it, too, differed from his remembrance. Sometimes when he'd been cramming for an examination and his mind had grown fuzzy, he'd tried bringing himself awake by remembering the single, rutted street and those two rows of false fronts, and he had been able to visualize each building in its proper place; and they were that way now. But the juice had been sucked from Ballardton, and it seemed a stupid sort of town, spiritless and dejected like those cattle glimpsed from the train.

He swung down and stood upon the depot platform, which was so hot that he could feel it through the soles of his shoes. He placed his telescope valise beside him and thumbed back his hat and mopped at his face with his handkerchief. He was a tall man with a rider's looseness giving him an easy grace, and he might have looked as though he belonged to this land, in spite of the black suit he wore, if the Eastern years hadn't taken the brown from his skin and the squint from his gray eyes. He had a dreamer's face, thin and sensitive; and his hair, thick and black, swept back from his forehead, making his brow higher. He stood here until he saw the buckboard round the depot and come to a halt, and the surprising thing to him was that the buckboard was pocketed by riders, and all of them wore guns.

He saw Wayne upon the buckboard's seat, and he watched his brother wrap the reins around the whipstock and come down to the ground, and he saw that all of Wayne's motions were slow and studied, and he wondered if the drought did that to people, too, sucking the juice from them and making them mechanical. He did a quick calculation and remembered that Wayne was only thirty-six — twelve years older than himself, but still too young to be so jaded, so burned-out looking. There was a stoop to Wayne's shoulders, and even his thin, sandy mustache looked tired. Moving toward Wayne, he thrust out his hand and said, "Hello, feller!"

Wayne took the hand and said, "Three days running we've met the train. You could have been more definite, Dan."

"There was some work I wanted to make up, Wayne. I didn't know how long it would take."

The riders were piling out of saddles; and Barney Partridge was the first of them to reach Dan. He was a little man, Partridge, short and stocky and warped by too much riding; he had been the Hourglass's foreman as long as Dan could remember, and he came forward now with a whoop and a holler and pounded Dan's back; and the others of the Hourglass crew spilled around Dan and made their exuberant greeting. Dan looked about for Cynthia and remembered there was no way of her knowing this would be the day, yet her absence bit into the man-pride of him. He said, to cover some awkwardness that bore no name, "I've got a trunk, Wayne. I see they've unloaded it."

Barney Partridge said, "We'll take care of the trunk, Daniel. It won't walk off meanwhile. This calls for a drink! Have you forgot what the inside of the Rialto looks like?"

Dan looked again at the guns they wore and wondered about that; this was not the 1870's when cattle, lean-flanked and long-horned, came spilling up the trail from Texas to Montana's virgin graze, and every man carried his law at his hip. He thought, *There was no need for all of them to come to meet me, but they did. Three days in a row. And they came gun-hung. What in the name of sense has happened to this range while I've been gone?*

But all he said was, "How's Gramp, Wayne?"

Wayne Ballard shrugged. "No better, no worse. Three years older than when you saw him last. I asked him if he wanted to ride into town and he cussed me out."

Barney Partridge said, "Do we have that drink or don't we?" and dragged at Dan Ballard's elbow.

10

They came around the corner of the depot, a compact, spur-jangling knot of men, and they crossed a short openness to the boardwalk and tramped along it. The smell of dust was heavy in the air; the unpainted siding of frame structures reflected the heat, and beat it back in steady waves. Flies buzzed about Ching Li's screened doorway; the heat before the restaurant was like a blast from a furnace, and the odor of sizzling steak smote a man like a club. They passed this establishment and the mercantile and Lily Greer's millinery and Ransome Price's land and loan office which had a *Back Soon* sign suspended from its doorknob. And all this became familiar to Ballard again, dissolving the thousand days between.

There were few horses at the hitchrails and few people on the street, yet Dan shook hands three times before they reached the Rialto. The saloon's hitchrail held six horses which stood with drooping heads, all of them bearing the Tomahawk brand; and when the Hourglass men set their feet to the warped steps leading to the porch beneath the wooden awning, the batwings spewed six riders.

At Dan's elbow, Wayne drew in a long, hard breath; and Dan felt the rigidity that laid hold on his brother.

Whatever else had changed, Old Man Cantrell hadn't, except that the ragged black beard which fell to his second shirt button now had a sprinkling of gray in it. He was a powerful man, thick of shoulder and thick of arm, with a barrel of a body mounted upon mighty legs. His five sons were at his back, and each had been cast from the mold of Old Man Cantrell. They were Rufe and Jeb and Mace and Ring and Hob — hill ranchers from the heights of the Rimfires, wild as that mass of mountains, untamed as the rivers that were born there. They held silent, leaving the speaking to their father, and that, too, was as it had been before. Old Man Cantrell had had more than a sociable drink, and the whisky blurred his tongue. He squinted hard against the blinding light and said, "Well, Daniel, so you've come back to Ballardton. Looks like they made a dude out of you back East."

Dan said, "I wonder."

"You're book-larned now, they tell it," Cantrell said. "Maybe you'll be able to pound some sense into Wayne's head." His squinted glance moved to the older brother. "You've got less than three days left," Cantrell said. "Saturday, midnight, is still the deadline."

Cantrell moved forward then, his sons trailing after him; they brushed hard against Dan in passing, and Dan knew a heady anger and fought it down. No one of this wild brood offered his hand, and that built a question in

Dan's mind, for there'd never been trouble between the Hourglass and the Tomahawk. You didn't make trouble for a Ballard in Ballardton. He saw the six pile into saddles and ruthlessly spur their horses to life; he saw them whirl the mounts and go thundering up the street, shooting raucously. He'd watched that spectacle a score of times in other days, but it had a new significance for him now. Why, they were a bunch of atavists — a throwback to the cave when a man did his hunting with a club and dragged his woman around by the hair! The anger went out of him and he smiled, wondering what Barney Partridge would have thought if the book-learned thought had been voiced.

The saloon was musty-dark and smelled sour, and when the Hourglass lined up at the bar, the bartender dragged his right hand across his apron and extended this moist paw to Dan. "Glad to see you back, Mr. Ballard," he said, and smiled a patronizing smile. "The drinks are on the house."

Dan tilted the bottle when it was passed to him and said, "Wayne, what's this about a Saturday-night deadline?"

Wayne gave a look around. Two men played a listless game of cards at a far table; against the wall another sat with a chair tilted back, his sombrero down over his eyes. "It will keep

13

until later, Dan. This is no place for talking."

Barney Partridge said, "Here's mud in your eye," and hoisted his drink.

The whisky tasted raw and savage to Dan; he felt out of tune with the place and the occasion. He wondered then if this was how it would be from here on, this feeling alien and removed from the things that had once been. Maybe now the dream of an endless, eternal land would be replaced by the remembrance of a campus and ancient halls and shade trees. Maybe the three years had sunk new roots down for him and there would be no transplanting, not again. Then he remembered the dreams and plans that were to come true because of those years, and he remembered Cynthia and tomorrow, and he remembered, too, the warm sincerity of the Hourglass's greeting at the depot, and he reached for the bottle again and said, "Boys, it's damn nice to be with you."

But his toast was lost in the creak of the batwings, and there was something so compelling about the man who entered that he drew Dan's eye and held it.

He was tall, and he was whiplash lean, this newcomer. He wore range garb and a flat-topped sombrero such as they favored in Utah; and his guns were thonged down against his thighs. He was young, no more than Dan's twenty-four, and there was a wild recklessness in him. All his features had a solidness to them, and his eyes were bleak and half veiled. He approached the bar with the quick stride of a man whose purpose is cut out for him, and he said, "You'd be Dan Ballard, eh? The pride of the tribe they named this town after. I'm Lew Fanshawe."

Dan said, "Is that supposed to mean something to me?"

Fanshawe's smile was a brief skinning of his lips from teeth that were startlingly white and perfect. "I'll grow on you," he said, "if you live long enough. And you will; your kind always dies in bed. I see you don't wear a gun."

The anger that Old Man Cantrell had inspired burst upward like a smoldering flame. "I could borrow one," Dan said.

One of Fanshawe's eyebrows twitched. "A Ballard with guts," he said. "I wouldn't have believed it! Or do you just *talk* big?"

Beside Dan, Wayne again drew in a long, hard breath and turned rigid, and it was Dan's thought that this was like a nightmare, horror-filled, lacking reality. A minute ago he had not known of this Fanshawe's existence, yet now they stood parrying words that could lead to only one ending. And with the realization that there'd been a studied intent to

Fanshawe's talk, a deliberate baiting, he knew also that there could be no side-stepping the issue. It was more than his anger that made this so; the inevitability was compounded of many things, but a man's pride was the greatest ingredient. Three years hadn't changed *that*.

Dan said, "When a man fetches me a fight, I expect him to fetch a good reason with it. I take it you've got your reason. Barney, pass me your gun!"

"*Dan* —" Wayne cried in a stricken voice.

"My gun's in my hand," Barney Partridge said coldly. "And it's lined on your brisket, Fanshawe. You were told to get off the Hourglass and stay off. Now I'm telling you to lay off us when we're in town. Git!"

Fanshawe looked beyond Dan and along the bar to where Partridge had stepped a pace away from the railing. Hourglass's foreman held his gun rigid; and Fanshawe smiled again and said, "I should have known I'd have the whole crew to buck. I'll see you later, Ballard."

He turned and walked easily toward the batwings, and they creaked with his departure. After that there was a long, heavy silence; even the pair at the table had ceased their card playing. Dan shook his head and said, "Did I dream it, or did it happen? What

16

made him pick on me?"

Wayne said quickly, "Come on, boys. Let's get out of here."

They pushed to the swinging doors and came through them and blinked in the strong sunshine, then stepped down to the board-walk. Lew Fanshawe had disappeared. A dog was picking his way from the far boardwalk, cutting diagonally across the street; in its exact center the dog chose to curl himself up and fall asleep. There was a naturalness to that little tableau that to Dan was somehow re-assuring; yet he plucked at Wayne's elbow and said, "You didn't answer my question about Fanshawe."

Irritation edged Wayne's voice. "What *can* I tell you? He's some drifting gunhand who hires out to whoever will pay him. He came to the Hourglass and offered his services. Barney ran him off the place. He's been sore at the outfit since. When he heard you'd come back, I suppose he saw a chance to make trouble."

"But why should he have tried to hire out to the Hourglass? We run a cattle ranch, not a shooting gallery."

Wayne said, "There's Cynthia."

He'd lifted his eyes, and Dan, following his gaze, saw the row of windows above the bank, the only two-storied building in town, and he saw the one window that bore the legend: QUINCY CHURCH, M.D. That window had been raised, and Cynthia was leaning from it. She said, "Hello, Dan," softly, sweetly, and he swept his hat away and held it in his hand and stood there, his eyes lifted and the sunlight strong in his face; and Wayne and the others ceased to be, for him.

Wayne said, "I'll meet you at the buckboard."

Dan crossed the street, his eyes still upturned, and he stumbled at the far boardwalk, then was into the covered stairway that clung to the side of the building. It was dark in here; the steps creaked with his weight, and he took them two at a time and burst into Doc Church's anteroom. Cynthia framed herself in the doorway of her father's office. He said, "Cyn! Ah, Cyn!" and came toward her with his arms open.

Behind her, Doc Church coughed discreetly, and Ransome Price said, "I'll be getting along."

In that first moment Dan had been aware of nobody but her. She wore a long, trailing dress of some rustling stuff that made her taller; these years had given her a filled-out roundness that stirred him deeply. Her bonnet dangled from her fingers, and her chin was high, and the golden glory of her hair was drawn back from her face to a neat bun at the nape of her neck. He had told her once, long ago, that she looked like something stamped upon an old coin, and this thought was strong in him; her features were a perfection of molding. She was coolness in a parched land, minted gold to an impoverished lover. She said, "It's good to see you again, Dan."

She was moving toward him; his lips went hunting hers and he managed to brush a kiss against her cheek. She linked her arm in his and drew him into the office; it was as he'd remembered it, a museum place of horsehair furniture, with a rolltop desk and a creaking swivel chair and a smell of medicines and disinfectants. Doc Church had put on weight, and his muttonchop whiskers had got grayer. He hoisted himself out of the chair and thrust a plump hand toward Dan and said, "It's good to have you back with us, boy. You remember Ransome Price."

Price stood leaning against the rolltop desk. He disengaged himself and offered his hand. "It's time you got here, Ballard," he said. "You should have wired that you were coming. Cynthia's had her best dress on every day of this week."

Dan said, "You're looking well, Price."

The man shrugged. He was as tall as Dan

and as lean, but he was nearer Wayne's age. He, too, wore a black suit and it fitted him well, and there was a heavy gold watch chain stretched across his vest. His face was sensuously handsome, and there was a studied affability to him. He said again, "I'll be getting along."

"You're kept busy these days?"

Price smiled. "With sixty rainless days to dry up everything but Ballard Springs. So, the bottom has dropped out of the land business. Everybody wants to sell — nobody wants to buy."

Dan said, "I'm sorry about not getting here sooner, Cyn. I should haye wired, I suppose. But I wasn't sure of the day until the last minute. We can rearrange plans since I got in so late."

"Tomorrow's the tenth, Dan," she said, her hand gentle upon his arm. "That's the day we set in our letters last spring. Everything is arranged — the church, Reverend Davidson, the invitations. You'll have Wayne for best man, of course. No, we'll be getting married tomorrow, just as we planned."

Price said, "You see, Ballard, you're getting that most priceless of possessions — an efficient woman. You have my congratulations."

"Thanks," Dan said, but suddenly the glory had dropped out of this moment. With Partridge and the others he had felt alien; there was a chasm of books and learning between the Dan Ballard they'd known and the Dan Ballard he'd become. Yet now he felt boorish and awkward and he was aware of the whisky smell that must be on his breath, and he wondered if that was why Cynthia had turned her cheek to him. And because there was nothing else he could find to say, he said, "Wayne's waiting for me at the depot."

"You're tired, of course," Cynthia said. "And probably hot and hungry. And you must be anxious to see Gramp. Run along now; we've got the rest of our lives for seeing each other."

Price had spoken twice of going, but still he stood beside the desk. What in hell was keeping him here, Dan wondered irritably. Didn't he suppose they'd want this moment to themselves? He drew the girl to him and kissed her. Price directed his attention to a corner of the room, and Doc Church fumbled with papers upon his desk. The kiss was fiercer than Dan had intended it to be; it was a reaching out, a yearning toward something he had wanted in this reunion and had not found. Cynthia laughed and said, "What a bear you are, Dan. Look what you've done to my hair!"

He found himself glad to be out of the room

and into the stairway. When he reached the boardwalk, Barney Partridge disengaged himself from a hitchrail where he'd been seated. "The others went on to the depot," Partridge said briefly.

And Partridge had stayed behind to make sure there would be at least one gun guarding him, Dan realized. Why was that?

They found Wayne seated in the buckboard, the reins in his hands. The others were up into saddles. The trunk had been loaded in the wagon. "Took two of us to lift it," Wayne said. "What are you carrying, Dan? Rocks?"

"Books," Dan said. "All the way to the bottom."

He climbed to the seat beside Wayne. His brother clucked the team into motion and brought the buckboard around. Dan said then, "I think the time has come for talking, Wayne. And I think you've got an awful lot to tell me."

2

Gramp Ballard

Out of Ballardton the land ran flat in all the directions, a sea of sage and yellowed grass made undulant by the haze of heat waves. To the north a road snaked toward the lift of the Rimfires, the mountains standing brown and drab and seeming always to recede, though on a day like this a man got the feeling that he could reach and touch the peaks with his hands. After the first mile, the Hourglass crew strung out, filing behind the buckboard and ahead of it, leaving the brothers in a pocket of dusty isolation. Wayne had kept his silence; he sat hunched upon the seat looking old and tired, and to Dan's patience he gave then this brief reply, "You want to know what the trouble's about. No rain. That's your answer."

"There's been nothing like it in our time," Dan said.

Wayne's shoulders twitched; he had never owned Dan's quickness of thought nor Dan's quickness of temper, but he had become a man drawn fine by adversity and there was a fiddle-string quality to him. He said, "About that Saturday night deadline, Old Man Cantrell wants to buy or lease Ballard Springs. He's given us until then to make up our minds."

Dan said thoughtfully, "So? It used to be that if any ultimatums were made on this range, the Ballards made them."

"Dad was alive then. And Gramp was able to sit a saddle."

"But nothing's changed, really, Wayne. The outfit that controls the water controls the range."

"Cantrell can see that, too," Wayne said with sudden savagery. "Add up the situation for yourself, Dan. We've got a river cutting down from the Rimfires, and it's the most useless river in creation, with those cliffs pocketing it so that a man can't haze his cattle to drink. We've got creeks, but all of them are dried up this season. And we've got Ballard Springs, and that's the only hope for everybody."

"Purgatory River has been on my mind many times," Dan said. "There's no sense in that water going to waste. There must be a way of raising it, of piping it to the Purgatory ranchers. I went into that matter at school. I've got plans, Wayne."

"And what good will they do us now?"

"Who cares about now? If Ballard Springs can weather the range through, we can plan for another season. There'll be other dry years."

"And there's the point," Wayne said. "Ballard Springs *can't* take care of everybody. Yet if it's shared and shared alike, all the ranchers will have cattle to ship come fall. I had Barney fence the springs off, Dan. I've been letting each of the ranchers water so many head a day. But that isn't good enough for the Cantrells. Old Man Cantrell wants all his cows on their feet come fall roundup. So he wants to own the springs. Yes, he's willing to put it on paper that the water will be shared even-Steven with the Hourglass. But it will be shut off to the rest of the ranchers."

"Cantrell isn't that wide across the britches, Wayne."

"But he is, Dan! That's the thing that's changed. Gramp and Dad were the first ranchers on the flats. You know that. They brought longhorns up from Texas after the war. Old Man Cantrell was the first rancher in the hills. He had a shirt-tail outfit to start with, but he built fast. Maybe a lot of Hourglass calves went into his gather in the old days. Gramp used to think so. But the point is that the Tomahawk is as big as we are. And Cantrell's got five sons. Once they were just so many hungry mouths to feed; now he's got five fighting men at his back. You saw him in town.

He isn't bowing and scraping before the Ballards these days."

Dan whistled softly. "So that's why a drifting gunhawk thought there might be work for him at the Hourglass."

"It's got the shape of a fight," Wayne admitted. "Fanshawe could have heard about that."

"And who's he hired out to now, Wayne? The Cantrells? Is that why he picked on me in the Rialto? Was I supposed to learn right off that the Ballards no longer walk high and mighty on this range?"

"I wouldn't know, Dan."

They fell silent; off to the right of the road was a prairie-dog village, but a whistling sentry had done his duty at first sight of an Hourglass rider and there were only so many mounds to be seen as they passed the spot. The land ran on endlessly before them, the tilt in it so slight as to be hardly discernible; and the sky arched above, blue and cloudless. The team stirred up small explosions of dust; it rose and became stifling, and Dan used his handkerchief again to mop his face.

Wayne said, "I could have put a great deal more than the drought into my letters, Dan. But you sounded like you were working hard this summer, and the trouble could keep. I'm glad you're back, kid."

26

Dan said, "Ransome Price? Is he up at Doc Church's a lot?"

Wayne kept his eyes ahead. "Maybe he's ailing, Dan."

"He looked healthy enough to me. And prosperous, too. Let's see, he came here about two years before I left. That makes him five years in Ballardton. He's grown, Wayne."

Wayne held silent. Then, "She's marrying you, just like the two of you planned, eh, Dan?"

"Tomorrow, Wayne. I supposed you knew."

"Then there's your answer, Dan. Yes, Price squired her a few places while you were gone. There aren't many people in Ballardton with the kind of background Doc's given Cynthia. You can't blame her for that, kid. Just remember it's you she's marrying."

"I wasn't worried."

"You plan on going ahead with the wedding, Dan?"

"Why not?"

Wayne gestured with his hand. "This trouble —"

Dan laughed. "The drought has made all of you a little crazy. The trouble's not as big as you think. Of course we're going ahead with the wedding."

Out of the silence that fell, Wayne said, a

27

mile later, "We're nearly home." Barney Partridge wheeled his horse and came back beside the buckboard, riding close to it and saying nothing. And then, suddenly, the land was falling away to a long reach below them; the slope had a caprock rim and was shale-mottled, and both Wayne and Dan had learned early gun-accuracy on the badgers that burrowed here. The Hourglass buildings were at the bottom of this slope, sheltered from the blizzard winds of winter; there was the high, red barn and the long, low bunkhouse, and the muddy sheen of a reservoir that had dwindled to almost nothing. Corrals, made from poles hauled from the hills, flanked the barn on either side. To the front stood the house, frame and two-storied and needing a coat of paint. A gallery ran the width of it along one side.

Looking, Dan thought, *Now I'm home.*

The slope was gentle; they wheeled down it and pulled to a stop before the ranch house; and when they leaped to the ground, one of the Hourglass hands led the team away for the unharnessing and the storing of the rig in the wagon shed. An ageless Chinese came to the cookhouse door, and Dan said, "Charley, you old sinner!" and ran to him and caught him and lifted him above his head.

Charley beamed. "I think you glowed up some, Dan."

Two dogs had come running, making a barking fury as the wagon wheeled into the yard, and one Dan remembered. He said, "Down, Ring! This is the only suit I've got and there's a wedding tomorrow. Where did this other fellow come from, Wayne? He's got a fine head on him."

"You remember Sam Digby's Girlie. She had three others just like him. Sam gave me the pick of the lot. I wrote you that Sam sold out, didn't I?"

Dan crossed to the gallery, climbed its steps, and opened the door. The big room into which he walked had a cavernous fireplace at its far end, and huge, hewn rafters overhead; and there was a scattering of hooked rugs and homemade furniture, some of it older than either of the brothers. These were the familiar, remembered things that made of a house a home; even the center table seemed to have the same stockmen's journals scattered upon it. Wayne, at his elbow, said, "We don't do bad for a bunch of bachelors."

"Where's Gramp?" Dan asked.

"Up in his room, I reckon."

Dan took the big stairs two at a time, and then stepped back to one certain spot he'd skipped in his rapid passage. It still creaked.

He smiled, and smiling came into the upstairs hallway and turned toward Gramp's room. The door was ajar, and he pushed at it with his hand and stepped inside. There were the bed and the chair and the same sort of hooked rugs, and there was the man in the chair. Dan said softly, "Hello, Gramp," and it came to him now that this was the one person above all that he'd wanted to see on coming home.

"Daniel," said Gramp Ballard and scowled. "What in hell did they do to you back there?"

They were alike, these two Ballards, far more alike than Dan and Wayne. They both had the tallness and the looseness and the thinness of face and height of forehead, but Gramp's hair was snowy white and so thin as to be an illusion of hair. The old man wore a fringed, buckskin shirt, open at the throat, and his legs were wrapped in a blanket, and a cane leaned beside him. Dan said, "Wayne wrote that you hurt yourself taking the rough off a cayuse. Are you able to get around?"

"Fair to middlin' with the cane," Gramp said. "Come closer, boy. *Shoes!* Are you too tender-footed for boots?"

"A pair of Justins wouldn't be much good for standing up in the aisle of a day coach, Gramp," Dan said. He saw now that his grandfather was older, much older; there was a grayness to those seamed, leathery features, a tiredness that was more than physical. He said, "It's mighty good to see you again, Gramp."

"And I suppose I ought to say that it's good to see you. But it isn't! Look at you! What have you been doing, frittering away all this time? Three years!"

Dan said patiently, "You know our plans, Gramp. We've wanted to make something bigger out of the Hourglass, taking up where you and Dad left off. That's why one of us had to get schooling."

"How much of the damn' alphabet did they tack onto your name?"

"I wasn't after a degree, Gramp, and I didn't get one. I took specialized courses and crammed four years' studying into three by staying through the summers. We're going to breed up better cattle, Gramp. I've learned all about that. I had one course in ranch accounting, and another in veterinarians' work. No, I don't qualify as a vet, but I'll bet I can cut down the percentage of loss we have from ailing cattle. Wait and see."

"Bah!" said Gramp. "Quit talking to me like I was a four-year-old kid or the town halfwit. Can you cure an ailing range of the trouble that's eating at it?"

"The trouble will vanish with the first rain, Gramp. You're all too excited about that.

31

Cantrell's bluffing. This isn't the day of the open range and the six-shooter. Old Man Cantrell can't turn back the clock."

"Ride up and tell him that!" Gramp snapped. "Tell him he's out of tune with the times. And tell those five giants he's brung up the same thing. They'll behave themselves once they learn that what they're doing ain't according to the books you've studied!"

It had killed Gramp to be tied here to a chair, Dan decided. That was it. Gramp never could stand inactivity, so he'd sat here and thought a lot of thoughts, and all of them had been bitter. The old fellow was glad to see him — of course he was! Gramp was just too die-hard stubborn to admit it.

Dan said, "I'm getting married tomorrow, Gramp. We'll fetch you to town to see it."

"Married?" Gramp said. "To the Church girl, I suppose. Why didn't you marry her three years ago, before you left? You were old enough, weren't you? If either of you gave a whoop for the other, you wouldn't have waited. You wouldn't have been able to."

"The schooling had been planned for me," Dan said. "It was Wayne's idea. Cynthia thought it was a good notion. We've got the rest of our lives ahead of us."

"Bah!" Gramp said. "You've never lived

and you never will. The Ballards are dying out."

"You'll live to see a great-grandson," Dan said.

"One bearing the Ballard name, yes," Gramp said. "But it won't have the Ballard guts. This range saw the last of those when your father died in the blizzard of '87. But maybe it ain't your fault, or Wayne's. Maybe the guts have died out of the land, and that's what makes the difference. Well, you're book learned. You'll get married and raise spineless children, and one year will be like another to you. You'll produce a better breed of cattle and a poorer breed of men. And you'll die at the end of it, and they'll tote you out to the Ballardton cemetery and give you a helluva good funeral, and you'll never even know what you missed. But maybe in the meanwhile Old Man Cantrell will change all that for you. Wayne will sell the springs to him, because Wayne hasn't the guts to buck him. And next he'll want one slice of our acreage and another, and he'll get those, too. I don't suppose you touched a gun all the time you were gone!"

Dan smiled. "I've got one in my trunk. I practiced every chance I got. You made that a habit with me. But gun-skill won't matter. Listen, Gramp —"

"No, *you* listen. And come closer. I want

33

to find out something."

Two steps brought Dan before the chair, and it happened then, so suddenly there was no preparing for it, no warning. The cane had been clutched tightly in Gramp's hand; it rose with startling quickness and came down hard across Dan's shoulder, a vicious blow. He stepped back instinctively, his hand going to his shoulder, and in him the fire of anger blazed brightly, but there was a sickness, too — a sickness of heart and soul. He thought, *He's gone crazy! That's it! He's an old man and this heat has cracked him!* And that took the anger out of him and he stood limply, his hands at his sides.

"Ah, Dan," Gramp said, and his face softened. "Just for a second you were mad enough to put your hands on my throat and choke the life out of me. Maybe there's hope for the Ballards yet. I had to find out, and there was only one way. I never laid a hand or a stick on you or Wayne before. I'm sorry, Daniel. And yet I'm glad."

"Forget it, Gramp. I'd take it from you. Any day."

The softness faded from the old man's face. "I guess it proved nothing," he said. He held silent a moment. "Don't marry her, Dan," he said then.

"I'm in love with her, Gramp."

"*Are* you? What in blazes do you know about love? Fifty-odd years ago I was a trader on the Sante Fe Trail. One night a bunch of Comanches run off my horses. I trailed them to their camp and watched them from a ridge. They had a girl, no more than fifteen, a prisoner from a wagon-train massacre. She was a slave to some buck, and in another year or so they'd have married her off to one of them. I took one look and knew what I had to do. I got her out of the camp that night — never mind how — and we were married by a black-robed padre the evening we hit Sante Fe. That's how a man behaves when he's in love. And the hell of it is, Dan, that sometimes when I look at you, I see her. You've got her black hair and her quick ways."

"It might have been that way with Cynthia and me, Gramp. But there was no Sante Fe Trail and no Comanches."

Gramp shook his head. "You don't even know what I'm talking about. If a girl's worth marrying, no man makes her wait three years. You haven't lived, Dan. You haven't known what it is to want a woman the minute you lay eyes on her and to know that nothing could be more important than marrying her — pronto. You haven't loved; and you haven't hated. Did you ever hate a man so much that nothing would satisfy you but to lay your bare hands on him? Just for a second you felt that way when I used the cane on you, but it didn't last. And you don't know what it is to believe in something — a cause, for instance, a cause so great that it's more important to you than living or dying."

"The Hourglass means something to me, Gramp."

"The Hourglass? Then Barney Partridge could have given you a better lesson than any you got from your Eastern teachers. He's out in the bunkhouse these days, eating his heart out because the spread he's worked for would rather side-step than fight Cantrell. Now do you see what I've had to sit here and watch day after day — the Ballard blood turned to water, the Ballard way of doing things lost forever. You were the last hope I had."

"You're thinking backward, Gramp. And looking backward, too. We've still a fight to make, and, in my own way, I've trained for that fight. There's blackleg to combat, and drought, and cattle losses."

Gramp turned his head and waved one hand. "Go away, Dan," he said. "Get out of my sight."

Downstairs, Wayne said with a wry grin, "I suppose you found him in his usual good humor. You look tired, Dan. Charley's got food on the stove, and your old room's ready for you."

Dan said, "I'll pass up the grub. I had something on the train."

"The wedding stolen your appetite, Dan? By this time tomorrow it will be over and done with."

The room was as Dan remembered it, and it was like Gramp's, but the bed somehow was not tempting. Nor was his trunk, which had been moved here. There were shelves for the books, and he might have unpacked. Instead he moved a chair to the window and sat with his elbows propped upon the sill, his chin cupped in his hands. The night came down from the Rimfires, the shadows running long and cool and purple, but the day's heat still clung to the house. The evening passed, and the lights bobbed out in the cook-shack and bunkhouse; but still Dan sat. A great moon rose to the east and made the yard day-bright; Barney Partridge came out of the bunkhouse, clad only in the long underwear he wore at all seasons. Hourglass's foreman had a drink at the pump, then sat beside it for a long time; and Dan wondered what it was that came between Partridge and his sleep until he remembered what Gramp had said about him.

Perhaps Dan dozed then. He had no remembrance of seeing Partridge return to the bunkhouse. But if he dozed he also awoke to doze again, and he stayed at the window and was there when the sun burst upon his wedding day.

3

Gunsmoke

All the old, familiar sounds tore the morning's silence asunder and brought Dan awake — the rattle of stove lids in the cook-shack, the crackle of the first fire, the intermittent creaking of the pump in the yard, the laughter and the banter of a crew jostling as they washed up. "Hey, cowboy," someone called, "don't hog the soap. It ain't *you* that's gittin' married." Horses stomped in the corral; one nickered softly. The scuffling of the crew aroused one of the dogs to a frenzy of barking. "Sure, you can borrow my best shirt, Pete," someone said distinctly. "You can just help yourself to it — *over my dead body*." The pump began creaking again, and further talk was lost.

The great house still held to night's hush. Dan came down the stairs to find Wayne burrowed in one of the chairs in the big living-room. Wayne said, "Morning, Dan. I didn't call you, figuring you needed the rest. Man, you look like you slept in your clothes!"

Dan combed his hair with his fingers. They were long fingers, and when their mother had been alive she had talked of a piano and les-

39

sons, but there had been a lean year or two, and the talk had been forgotten. Dan said, "When Charley gets the crew fed, I'd like him to heat enough water for a bath. While I'm taking it, he can run an iron over this suit."

He breakfasted alone; Wayne had already eaten, and busied himself out in the yard. Charley got the big tin bathtub from a shed and placed it on the kitchen floor, and when Dan stripped down and eased himself into the water he could hear Charley in the next room, toiling with his ironing board and singing lustily. Dan worked a lather out of the harsh, homemade soap. Charley sang, "Onward Clistian soldiers, marching as to wa-ll —"

Dan had forgotten how hard Montana's water was, but at least it took the grime off him and the tiredness out of his muscles. Splashing, he reflected that here was the stuff that caused all the trouble. You drank it and you bathed in it and you fought over it. And then he had to grin at his next thought. You were supposed to hope for a sunny, cloudless day for your wedding, and he was wishing it would rain.

Wayne came in when Dan had got dressed again. Wayne said, "I had the buckboard hitched. You and me will ride in it. The crew will come by saddle horse."

"Wearing guns?"

Wayne said, "We figure it best, kid. Till this matter gets settled with Cantrell. And there's Lew Fanshawe, too, remember."

"No guns," Dan said firmly. "Cynthia wouldn't like it. Is Gramp coming along?"

"I asked him this morning," Wayne said forlornly. "He cussed me out."

"Is that all?"

"No, he said something foolish. He said there were two things he couldn't abide — fancy weddings and fancy funerals. And this affair, in his opinion, is both. You mustn't mind him, Dan. He makes very little sense these days."

"I wonder," Dan said.

Wayne shrugged. "You look all shined and proper, kid. Best looking groom in a month of Sundays. I hope I don't fumble the ring."

"Ring! Wayne, I didn't get a ring! Do you suppose I can buy one in Ballardton?"

"Cynthia got the ring, kid. She said it would be just like you to forget. I've been toting it for a week. But you'd better switch back to those shoes you were wearing yesterday. You won't need riding boots in the buckboard."

"These feel more comfortable, Wayne. I had Charley dig them out of my room. At least my feet haven't grown since I left."

Wayne shrugged again. He, too, was wearing store clothes today, but that stoop was still in his shoulders, and the tiredness was still in his face. And from the sight of him there was born a quick sympathy in Dan, and for a moment they were close, very close. Dan said, "I forgot to find out the time of the wedding, too. I guess no groom ever needed a best man worse than I do."

"High noon," Wayne said. "We'd better get going. I'll tell the boys about the guns. Come along when you're ready."

The buckboard had been fetched before the house. When Dan climbed to the seat, he said, "Let me handle the reins today. I don't think I've lost the knack." He kicked off the brake, and they went clattering up the slope.

Wayne said, "Remember how Gramp used to bring us here and have us bang away at the badgers? It's a wonder we didn't grow up lopsided from carrying the weight of six-shooters before we were knee-high to the pump. Seems kind of crazy now."

But Dan wasn't so sure. They'd got to be men themselves and they figured Gramp for an old fool who didn't know that yesterday was forever gone. But maybe he'd seen all this coming, seen it away off. Maybe that was why he'd schooled his grandsons the way he had.

The road leveled off, and he let the horses

gait themselves to a gallop; it was good to feel the tug of them against the reins, to sense the power a man commanded when he governed a team of horses. Strong light gave a sharpness to the range; dew bediamonded the browned grass, and they could see Ballardton across the distance, etched clearly in the first sunlight. They came again to the prairie-dog village, and again the rodents were gone from sight. Behind the wagon the crew strung out; there was an early morning zest in men and horses. But the sun climbed higher and took on heat, and Dan slackened the pace of the team. Now the dust began rising, and across the flatness they could see where other roads converged upon the town; dust laid its plumes along all these roads.

"Everybody's turning out for the wedding, looks like," Wayne said.

"Cynthia must have sent a lot of invitations."

"She talked to me about that," Wayne said. "She didn't invite the Cantrells. Or the new fellow who took over Sam Digby's place."

Barney Partridge came galloping up beside the buckboard and shouted something that was lost in the rattle of wheel and hoof; he was freshly shaved today and wearing his Sunday best, but beneath the skirt of a coat that had once been black and had turned bottle-

43

green with age, the handle of his six-shooter peeped. Seeing this, Dan frowned, and Wayne spread his hands in a flat gesture. "I told them," Wayne said. "Most of them went back to the bunkhouse and shucked their guns. I guess Barney didn't hear me."

"He heard you," Dan said.

All this was lost upon Partridge; he grinned a wide grin and went galloping up ahead and led the way into Ballardton. The town had taken on an election-day look; every hitchrail was crowded to capacity, and buckboards and buggies lined the street, sometimes two deep, choking the narrow way. The boardwalks were banked with people, some merely standing and waiting, some milling aimlessly. Dan steered the buckboard between Sully Gant's blacksmith shop and the White Elephant livery stable, finding an empty space in this weedy lot.

"We can walk to the church from here," he said.

The crew had dispersed, each man seeking out a hitchrail for himself. They gathered again as the brothers reached the boardwalk; they pocketed the two, and the group moved up the street. Dan found himself seeking a glimpse of Cynthia; he raised his eyes to the window of Doc Church's office, but that window was blank today. She would be at the church, he supposed; wasn't there some superstition about bride and groom seeing each other before the wedding? Yesterday's fleeting hunger was in him; he wanted the nearness of her, yet there was a faint shadow of uncertainty now; and Gramp Ballard had cast that shadow.

And, thinking of this, Dan found himself appraising for the first time his real attitude toward Cynthia, and wondering what inexorable steps had brought him here today. Cynthia had long been part of his life; he'd liked her, and, a few years ago, he'd fancied himself as her pursuer, yet it had been Cynthia who'd first mentioned marriage. Thereafter the match had somehow become a settled matter, though once a townsman had intimated that a girl was no fool who married a half-interest in the Hourglass and Dan had struck him, making this violent reply to the insinuation that Cynthia was shrewd and calculating. Loyalty was ingrained in him, but now he wondered if loyalty, rather than love, was sending him to the altar, and if his eagerness for her yesterday, had merely been that time had turned backward at first sight of her. Would he feel differently now if Ransome Price weren't so obviously interested in Cynthia?

Barney Partridge said, "Time enough for a drink, from the looks of the sun. Yonder's the Rialto. Come on, Dan; we'll get you something to take the shakes out of your knees."

It was in Dan to make an easy refusal; he was still remembering yesterday and how Cynthia had turned her lips away from him because the smell of whisky was on his breath. And then, suddenly, he sensed that all the rest of his life would be this way, choosing between the man he'd been and the man he'd become once the wedding ceremony was performed. And because there were many things to which a man had to remain true, he said, "Just one, Barney. And we'll have to down it quick."

"*Yipee-ee!*" Barney shouted, and cut diagonally across the dust toward the saloon, the others following him.

And that was how Dan came face to face with Lew Fanshawe, who leaned indolently against one of the posts supporting the wooden awning fronting the Rialto.

There was that easy grace to Fanshawe, and that wild recklessness, too. His eyes were as bleak as before, and half veiled, but there was a mocking devil in them. He was like some great tawny cat taking its ease in the sun; he showed those teeth of his, so startlingly white, so startlingly perfect, and he said, "Happy the groom the sun shines on today, Ballard. You look as polished as a new spur. She'll be getting quite a man. Quite a man."

Dan said, "Fanshawe, I want no trouble today."

Fanshawe detached himself from the support, removed his flat-topped sombrero, and made a sweeping bow. "A Ballard has spoken," he said. "That makes it the law in town, eh? But here's a little wedding present for you."

He worked his lower lip quickly and spat then, spat upon the toe of Dan's right boot. And suddenly there was silence all around, silence and immobility, the talk dying among those who lounged within hearing distance, and every man growing roots where he stood. And the anger that burned in Dan was first a quick flame, rising, searing, all-consuming, and then it was a cold flame, leaving ice in him, and a feeling as though he were detached from himself. He said in a voice that sounded like someone else's, "Barney, give me your gun and belt."

Partridge said hoarsely, "He's stepped too far this time! He'll ride out of here on a rail, wearing a coat of tar and feathers."

"Barney! Give me your gun!"

Abe Potter came shouldering through the crowd. He was Ballardton's town marshal, a big and ponderous man, made more ponderous by the badge he wore. He had held this position as long as Dan could remember, and it had been three years since they'd seen each other, but this was no time for greetings. Potter's florid face showed the weight of his anger. He said, "I saw it. I saw it all. He'll get thirty days for disturbing the peace."

Fanshawe measured Potter with a cool scorn. "And who'll make the arrest, fat man?"

Potter shrank visibly, then found a source of courage. "I can make a deputy of every man on the street."

Fanshawe said, "You're well covered, Ballard. Yesterday it was your crew behind you. Today it will be the whole town. Yes, she'll be getting quite a man!"

Dan said, "The gun, Barney!"

He reached out with his right arm, never taking his eyes from Fanshawe, and Partridge unlatched his gun belt and passed it over, and Dan swung it around his waist and hooked it in place and patted the gun into position against his thigh. Wayne said, "Dan! You don't have to do this!"

Yes, I do, Wayne. That was his thought. He had to do this because if he didn't stand up to Fanshawe today, he'd have to face him tomorrow or the day after, or the shadow of Fanshawe would be over him all the days to come. He had to do it because somebody wanted it done — this man before him or some other man behind him, whispering in Fanshawe's ear. There wasn't any choice.

He fell back a step, making a spreading gesture with his hands, and the crowd began dissolving, leaving him a breadth of space as men hurried to the cover of doorways. He fell back another step and another, still keeping his eyes on Fanshawe, and yet there was an awareness in him that all the others had put themselves at a safe distance, and that was the way he wanted it. He kept backing until the calves of his legs struck against the edge of the far boardwalk; and he looked across the intervening space at Fanshawe and said, "This should be about right," and let his hands dangle limply at his sides.

Fanshawe had put on his hat and slanted it against the sun and taken a spread-legged stand on the porch of the Rialto. The grin was gone and the mockery was no longer in the man's eyes; he was all business now, and it was deadly business.

And with the two of them thus, each ready to kill the other, Dan sensed again his own detachment from all this, and he wondered if this was what Gramp had meant about hating a man so much that you wanted to lay your bare hands on him. Yet there was no hate in Dan, not really, and when he saw the flicker of Fanshawe's eyes and knew the signal for what it meant, he merely let his hand reach toward his right hip, remembering Gramp and the badgers then and being thankful for the stolen hours of practice at school; and he got the gun out and eared the hammer back all in the same motion. He heard the roar of Fanshawe's gun, but Fanshawe was just a shade too confident and that was why the bullet merely whispered past Dan's ear. And then Dan was firing.

No, there was no hate. And that was why, at the last moment, he tilted the gun a little to the left and raised it a fraction of an inch. He felt the buck of it against his palm; he saw Fanshawe go spinning about, the gun falling from the man's fingers as shock took its hard hold on him, and he saw Fanshawe's hand go to his right shoulder and the blood come seeping between his fingers.

Abe Potter moved fast for a fat man. He had posted himself at the far end of the Rialto's porch; he came running now and he kicked at Fanshawe's gun and sent it spinning and dragged Fanshawe's left-hand gun from its holster and threw it after the fallen gun. Then he got a hold on Fanshawe's elbow and hustled the man down the steps. The crowd came converging from everywhere; there was anger in the air and it manifested itself in shouted curses and lifted voices. Potter said, "Back, everybody! He's the law's prisoner!" He beat a lane for himself, dragging the stunned Fanshawe behind him; and Barney Partridge scooped up Fanshawe's fallen guns and was there helping Potter.

Wayne reached Dan's elbow. He said, "You'd better get up to the church to Cynthia. The news will have gone ahead of you."

Somebody said, "She's already heard it."

Dan moved blindly up the street, his boots raising little geysers of dust. Men spoke to him, and he shook his head, not always comprehending. Someone came running, and said, "Miss Church fainted. They've carried her to her father's office."

Dan turned and headed toward the covered stairway, and Wayne went with him. They climbed the stairs together, and when they reached the office, Cynthia lay stretched upon the horsehair sofa, her long white dress in disarray, her veil thrown back, her eyes still closed. Doc Church was fussing over her, and Ransome Price stood in attendance. He was the one who'd carried Cynthia there, Dan guessed, and he wondered then if the man would always be underfoot. A great annoyance gave a petulant cast to Price's face. He said, "Ballard, couldn't this thing have been avoided today of all days?"

Dan said, "No, it couldn't."

Doc Church was passing smelling salts beneath Cynthia's nose. Her eyelids fluttered, lifted; she saw Dan and closed her eyes again, tightly. He stepped nearer and said, "It's all right, Cyn. It's all over now, and I'm still in one piece."

Her bouquet had fallen to the floor beside the sofa. It was a big bouquet, full and rich and many colored, and these were flowers foreign to this soil. Dan wondered where they had come from until he realized they were made of paper. Artificial.

Doc Church was perspiring, and his wing collar and tie were awry. He said, "I'm afraid the sight of you brings back the shock, Dan. She'll be all right shortly."

Dan said, "We can tell the crowd the wedding will be delayed an hour or so."

"You're going through with it?" Price demanded.

"If Cyn wishes it."

"She'll wish it. She's that kind of thoroughbred, Ballard. Yes, she'll marry you. Even if that kill-crazy fellow is out of jail in thirty days and makes a widow of her."

Dan said wearily, "Wayne, go tell the crowd the wedding's been postponed. Indefinitely."

"It doesn't have to be that way, kid," Wayne said gently.

"Yes, it does," Dan said. "Price is right.

52

I can't marry her as long as there seems to be some kind of curse hanging over me. I can't do that to her, even though she'd be willing. Go tell the folks, Wayne."

Wayne turned and left, and Dan said then, futilely, "I guess I'll be going, too. Back to the ranch probably. Tell her I'll ride in and see her later. Maybe tonight."

Price said, "You'd better get that thing out of sight. That's what scared her when she opened her eyes."

Only then did Dan realize he was still clutching Barney Partridge's six-shooter in his right hand. He slid the weapon into the holster and turned toward the stairs.

4

The Spark
and the Powder

They sat in rawhide-bottomed chairs upon the gallery, the two of them, Wayne and Dan; they had been here since suppertime. They had seen the shadows come down from the hills and engulf the Hourglass; the day had lost its heat and all things had turned hazy and out of focus. A breeze still ran over the land, but lazily and without malice, having coolness in it now, having a caress. Wayne kept Durham and papers in his pocket, and Dan had again tried his hand at the fashioning of a cigarette and found an old skill still in his fingers. He'd favored a pipe at school. He was like an Indian, he reflected, educated and returned to the reservation and gone native overnight. But he smiled at the thought. Ring came padding up on the gallery and approached Dan and asked in subtle, silent ways to be nuzzled. The two cigarettes made pin points of light against the gathering night.

Wayne said with a tired sigh, "It was quite a day. Quite a day!"

"I think I'll ride in," Dan said. "There's

this thing to talk over with Cynthia. And I'd like a word with Lew Fanshawe. But it will be wasted jaw-wagging, I reckon. He'll never tell who hired his gun."

"The Cantrells," Wayne said, but not with conviction.

"I wonder, Wayne. They've got guns of their own. There'd be that kind of pride in Old Man Cantrell, the kind that would make him keep a fight in his own family."

"He'll be down soon for his answer, kid."

There was a question in that statement, a question and an appeal; and Dan knew now that Wayne had waited for his return, wanting his backing and his judgment, and that seemed odd. It was as though an older brother had suddenly become a younger one. Yet, because this was still unbelievable, Dan said, "And what is your answer going to be, Wayne?"

Wayne carefully ground out his cigarette, setting his heel upon it and making sure the last spark was extinguished. He made a ritual of this. "The whole range is counting on Ballard Springs," he said then. "But are we always going to have to play godfather to every two-bit spread in the basin? We've shared the water, sure; but this is a season where every man's for himself. There'd be enough for us and Cantrell, and if we made a dicker with Cantrell that would be straight business. The little fellows might not like it, but they couldn't blame us."

Dan said softly, "And that's how you see it?"

"It's that or fight, Dan. Maybe we should have hired Fanshawe after all. Maybe it isn't too late. Unless you want to make some kind of charge against him, he won't draw more than thirty days for disturbing the peace. And who would we be fighting for, when it comes right down to it? Ourselves? Cantrell will share and share alike with us. Why should the Hourglass keep on riding gun-hung so that we can have the privilege of giving our water away to all the others?"

"And if we lease the springs to Cantrell?" Dan said. "What next? He'll be after a slice of our acreage, and he'll get that, too, and then he'll be after another." It came to him suddenly that he was saying the very thing Gramp had said, and, remembering that, he added, "Gramp has a vote in this, too, Wayne."

"Which could make it two against one. You and Gramp against me. I think he's been counting on that ever since you started home. He'll vote to tell Cantrell to go to hell and to fight the Tomahawk if they don't like it. You know better than that, Dan. The day of the gun is gone."

"Is it?" Dan said, and remembered the silent street and the breadth of space and the noon sun strong in his face, that and the flicker of Fanshawe's eyes.

"Today?" Wayne scoffed. "There'll always be a few like Fanshawe until time stamps the last of them out."

"Shall we tell Cantrell that?" Dan asked, not meaning to put an edge to his voice.

"*Shhhh!*" Wayne said suddenly, and his fingers, closing on Dan's arm, compelled silence.

Dan heard it, too, the sound of a walking horse, the jingle of a bit chain out there in the darkness, the creak of saddle leather. Wayne was leaning forward, a rigidity to his body, and it came now to Dan that fear was strong in Wayne and had been with him for a long time. Dan said, "One of our crew, likely."

"No, they'll be coming in a bunch. They had themselves primed to celebrate a wedding, you know. When it was called off, I told them to spend the day in town anyway. We'll see none of them before midnight."

Out yonder, saddle leather creaked again, and a man dismounted and shaped up in the yard. He was a tall man, thin and built along angular lines. He came toward the house with a sureness in his step; he wore bibless overalls with crisscrossing suspenders, and a sombrero

57

was shoved back on his head, and there was a rifle in the crook of his arm. His face was clean-shaven, and the sun had done little to him; there was a strained grayness to his face, and his lips were thin and bloodless. His nose was an aristocrat's nose, and his eyes were coldly intelligent. He stood at the front of the steps, revealed in a splash of lamplight from the open doorway behind Wayne, and he said, "Good evening, gentlemen." His voice was the most astonishing thing of all — softly modulated, cultured.

Wayne said, "Good evening. Do I place you right? You're Allison, the fellow who took over Sam Digby's outfit up by the pass?"

"Clayton Allison," the man said. "I've never had the pleasure of your acquaintance, but you're Wayne Ballard, of course. And this is your brother Dan, I presume." His tone was sardonic, making a mockery of the courtliness of his words. He didn't step forward to offer his hand.

Wayne said, "Come on up and have a chair, Allison. What can we do for you?"

Allison lowered the rifle and leaned upon it, making no other move than that. "I'm looking for my daughter. We'll dispense with any sparring with words, gentlemen. Is she here?"

Wayne spread his hands in a gesture of bewilderment. "I didn't even know you had a daughter. Why should she be here?"

"Because there are men here. You have a large crew, Mr. Ballard. And then there are yourselves, gentlemen."

Wayne frowned. "I'm not exactly sure what you mean, but I don't think I like it. We've seen nothing of your daughter. What does she look like?"

"She's nineteen. Usually she wears Levis and a shirt, and she might pass for a boy, but only at a distance. Her hair is black and hangs to her shoulders. Her eyes are black. She's pretty — as pretty as the devil's daughter would be if he had one."

"If she shows up, we'll let her know you're hunting for her."

"In the meantime," Allison said, "I'll have a look in your bunkhouse, if you don't mind."

"In our bunkhouse? What in hell for?"

"For her, of course. Maybe your men have hidden her out. She could twist any man around her finger." His eyes were suddenly savage. "It's an inherited trait."

Wayne said hotly, "Look in the bunkhouse and be damned to you, if it will make you feel any better. What kind of a ranch do you think we run here?"

Allison dipped his head. "My apologies," he said. "If I make them with a reservation, it's because I realize that you don't know April."

Dan said quietly, "Most of the range folks were in town today. A lot of them stayed. Maybe your girl's there."

Something touched Allison's lips that might have been a smile. "I've already heard about your wedding and its postponement. Be wise and postpone it indefinitely, Mr. Ballard."

Dan came to a quick stand, his hands making fists. "Now see here —" he declared.

Allison moved the rifle back to the crook of his arm. "I meant no personal offense," he said. "I've never met Miss Church, but I'm told that she's most reputable. My views on marriage are my own. You're young, Mr. Ballard. Someday you'll remember my words and understand them."

He turned and headed back toward his horse. He took three steps and paused, swinging about on his heel. "Your north line fence has a hole in it," he said. "Some of your stock drifted through onto my land. I hazed them back and patched the fence as best I could. I'm not very adept at that sort of thing. You'd better have it attended to properly."

Wayne said, "I'll get a man up there soon. And thanks, Allison. If it happens again, just get us word. We'll save you the bother of having to round up our stock."

"It wasn't a favor to you," Allison said. "I just didn't want your crew swarming over my land. But I've forgotten. You don't know my daughter, do you?"

He went on to his horse; they heard him climb into the saddle and wheel the mount about; man and beast became shapeless and were lost in the night, only the hoofbeats reaching back to the brothers. Dan sighed, not knowing whether to laugh or be angry. "Now where in thunder did he come from?" he demanded. "And what eats him? For a while I thought he was drunk, but his eyes were too clear and his step too steady."

Wayne said, "He took over Digby's place this spring. He's no rancher, not by a long shot, though he runs a little stock back in the hills. Minds his own business strictly. This is the first time I've ever come face to face with him, though he was pointed out to me once in town. He comes down every thirty days or so for supplies, pays cash and talks to nobody. I never even knew he had a daughter, and I don't think many others know it either."

Dan said thoughtfully, "The Digby place. That wedges between us and the Tomahawk, and it overlooks Tomahawk Pass. How are you betting Clayton Allison will line up if it comes to a war?"

"I don't know," Wayne said. "I just don't know."

Dan shrugged the matter aside. "Pass over those makings again," he said. "One more smoke and I'm saddling up to ride to town." He took the sack and let a pinch of tobacco dribble into the paper. "Was a time when my biggest ambition was to be able to do this with one hand. Like Gramp could."

"He's getting worse," Wayne said. "Now he's throwing things. I went upstairs after Charley fetched him his supper. I thought he'd like to hear about today. He shied a boot at me."

"Allison's coming back," Dan said.

Again a horse was shaping up at the gate; the stars were beginning to show now and it was lighter, and on the heels of his words Dan knew his mistake. That short and stocky form was Barney Partridge's. Hourglass's foreman came to the gallery and squatted upon the steps. Wayne said, "Getting too old to stand the pace, Barney? Time was when you'd fetch the crew home and put 'em to bed, then head back to town to finish your own liquoring."

Partridge silently extended his hand and Dan passed him the makings. He tilted the sack, spilling never a crumb; he twisted the cigarette into shape and ran his tongue along it. He fished for a match, raised a leg and drew the match along the seat of his trousers. For a moment his face was painted brightly against the gloom; he got the tobacco burning, and he said then, "They're fixing to lynch him."

"Lynch who?" Dan demanded.

"Fanshawe."

"*Fanshawe!*" Dan came to his feet again. "*Who's* talking of lynching him?"

"The whole town. Or them that's liquored enough to be of a mind for it. I heard the talk grow all afternoon. First it was of tar and feathers and a rail. You'll mind that I mentioned something of the sort this morning myself. Then it turned to talk of a battering ram for the jail door and a rope and a cottonwood and a quick dance on the air."

Wayne said hoarsely, "A lynching in Ballardton?"

"Folks set a store in the family," Partridge said. "They're beholden to the Ballards for all the things over all the years. Right now they're especially beholden with no water on this range but Ballard Springs. They figger Dan got himself cheated out of a wedding because of Fanshawe. They figger a funeral might square that."

Dan said, "You've all gone crazy! Do you hear? You've all turned loco! A lynching! A good sprinkle to settle the dust and this craziness would be washed out of you!"

He vaulted over the railing, landing hard. Wayne came to a stand then. "Where are you going, Dan?"

"To town," Dan said. "Just as fast as I can saddle up! Do you think I want to spend the rest of my life remembering a man dead because of something that happened between him and me? I'm going to talk some sense into those misguided fools!"

"The time for that is past, I reckon," Barney Partridge said. "Hours past. Whisky bottles past. You've never seen a lynch mob, Dan."

Dan said, "Then here's one I'm going to see — and stop. I want Fanshawe alive! I want to get a truth out of him that will maybe put an end to whatever it is that's hanging over my head. But it isn't Fanshawe that matters. Not tonight. Can't the two of you see what this really means? The drought has made some folks crazy enough to be thinking of a lynching. But if Fanshawe's hanged tonight, that will just be a start. Supposing Cantrell's behind the man? Do you think he'll let the lynching be the end of it? This is just the spark. It's the powder keg I'm thinking of!"

He went running toward the corral. Behind him, Partridge's voice reached out through the night. "Hold up a minute, Dan. If you're fool enough to try stopping it, I'm fool enough to ride along and help you. Wait till I get me a fresh horse."

5

Back in the Saddle Again

Partridge shaped up out of the darkness, leading his spent saddler toward the corral. He peeled the saddle from the mount and let the kak lie, and he turned the horse into the corral and lifted his lariat from the tangle of heaped gear. He said, "You still got my gun, Dan? Better fetch it and one for yourself. Some in town are your friends, wanting to square the insult that was tossed at you. Some are soreheads, grabbing this as a chance to see how a man looks at the end of a rope. We can't stand up to them with our bare hands."

Dan did some rummaging in the bunkhouse and found a pair of spurs which he fastened to his heels; and he fetched back two gun belts, the one around his middle, the other in his hand. Partridge had laid his loop on two horses and got his own saddle onto one of them and was fetching another kak from the harness shed. He slapped this saddle across the back of a bay gelding. "I hand-picked this one for you, Dan," he said. "If you're three years out of practice, you'll want an easy handful the first time."

Dan said, "Is he fast? That's all I care about."

"He'll get you there and back," Partridge said.

They stepped up into saddles, and Dan put his weight in the middle and was glad now that he still wore riding boots. He'd have to get used to this all over again. He'd be stiffer than a board tomorrow. But it was good being back in the saddle again. It was good to have a horse under you. It gave you wings and made you look down on lesser men. If you were born to it, you never got it out of your blood. Back East they were talking about those new horseless carriages, and some said that in a few more years the horse would be gone. It wouldn't be so, Dan reflected. Not as long as there were Ballards.

Hourglass's foreman leaned and closed the corral gate; they wheeled their mounts and lifted them to a gallop and crossed before the ranch house as they headed south. Wayne still stood on the gallery. He shouted something at them; but it was lost in the rising thunder of hoofbeats. Wayne had made no move to come along. Wayne wanted no part of violence, Dan decided. Wayne closed his eyes to it and pretended it didn't exist.

They humped over the top of the slant

and the prairie ran level and unbroken before them; starshine silvered the sage and gave to the land an ethereal look. They kept to the wagon road; there were always prairie-dog holes for the unwary; and the wind of swift passage grew in Dan's ears and the taste of it was on his lips and was good. It came to him that he hadn't lived these past years. He'd turned himself into a mechanical man involved with books and learning, but now he was taking up where he'd left off and it was like being born again. And it came to him also that he hadn't come home until this hour, not really. It was the difference a saddle horse made to a range-reared man.

They rode stirrup to stirrup, holding to a high gallop, and the prairie blurred past them and was endlessly the same. Yonder, across the miles, lay Ballardton, and sometimes Dan fancied he could make out the huddle of buildings, but he knew this was an illusion born of expectancy. Only the lights were real. Midway to town, as Dan calculated it, Partridge pulled to a halt, dismounted, and loosened the cinch of his saddle, letting the horse blow, and Dan did likewise. In this brief recess, Dan said, "There's been a question pestering me, Barney. You were in town and knew what was happening. But it didn't matter to you one way or the other, and you rode out. Now you're backing me in whatever play is to be made. Why, Barney?"

Partridge gave this his careful consideration and the labor of thinking showed in his leathery face. "I dunno," he said at last. "Maybe in town I figgered it was none of my business, one way or the other. Then when you spoke of how a lynching might be just a beginning, I saw it different. Hell will bust out soon enough without giving it a headstart."

A good man, Dan reflected. Partridge's way had been to take orders, to let the Ballards do the thinking, but when he got his teeth into a notion you could count on his backing you till his belly caved in. The Hourglass was lucky to have him. Damned lucky!

Partridge fumbled with the cinch. "Time's a-wastin'," he observed.

Then they were riding again, and shortly Dan knew that he could indeed make out the huddle of buildings. First he identified the church spire and the blotch of darkness against darkness beneath it, and, as they drew nearer, the blotch took on shape and substance and became the town. When they rode into the street, there were still more buckboards and saddle horses here than usual, though the town had lost its crammed look of the morning. They racked their horses at the first hitchrail that would accommodate them, and they stood then for a moment indecisively. Dan wondered if they were too late, if the thing had already been done, and the thought took the rigidity out of his knees.

"Just listen to 'em," Partridge said. "They're set for the kill."

The Rialto was the nearest saloon; from it came a splash of light that lay upon the boardwalk and made the dust beyond something yellowish and alive. A low and constant rumble boiled from the saloon, the blending of many voices, and there was a note in it that a man, hearing once, would never forget. It was compounded of anger and hate and a nameless blood-hunger; it was made from the latent violence in men and the searing touch of sixty rainless days. Farther up this same street was the Gilded Lady, and across the way stood the Palace. The same voice came from each; men were liquoring in all three saloons. The hour was near. And yet there was an unreality to this; violence didn't blossom in Ballardton, not any more. The town had outgrown a turbid past and now it was reverting; and that was the unbelievable.

Barney Partridge shifted his gun to a more comfortable position, and the gesture was real enough.

"You figger to make them a speech?" he asked.

"From the jail steps," Dan said, and not until now had he had a plan. "It's the only way. If I go into one of the saloons, I'm likely to be still talking when they start marching from another."

"Where do I fit into it, Dan?"

"Wander around the saloons and keep an eye on things, Barney. If anybody gets ready to explode, run to the jail and fetch me the news. There's a light in Potter's office, I see. Maybe he's got a notion or two on how to stop this thing."

Partridge spat into the dust. "Maybe," he said, but there was no conviction behind it. He climbed to the boardwalk, and his boot heels beat a cadence along it; he shouldered among men and was lost to Dan's sight.

Turning toward the jailhouse, Dan cut diagonally across the dust and, in this manner, passed before the Palace. Horses stood here; he read the Circle-Bar's brand and the Hashknife's and the Wagon Wheel's; these were near neighbors who depended upon Ballard Springs, and owed the Hourglass allegiance. A few men loitered beneath the saloon's awning; the batwings parted and a man stood silhouetted, a big and ungainly man, and by his bulk Dan knew him to be Old Man Cantrell. You couldn't mistake Cantrell. He was like a boulder, solid and impregnable. He stood looking out upon the street, and if he saw Dan he gave no sign. The batwings creaked again and a second giant shaped up behind the first. This was one of Old Man Cantrell's sons; he stood at his father's elbow and said something, and the two turned back into the saloon.

Here, then, was the living proof that the Tomahawk was in town, and Dan's first thought was that if Cantrell money had hired the gun of Lew Fanshawe, then Cantrell and his sons could be counted on to help stop the thing that was shaping in poured whisky and rumbling talk. But there was no real satisfaction in the Tomahawk's presence in town. Now there was the one faction and the other, and from this proximity could come the beginning of a war. Better that Lew Fanshawe should die than that the Cantrells should be here to defend him.

Dan reached the boardwalk and began pacing along it. The jail was toward the outskirts of town, isolated and removed from other buildings by a futile belief that Ballardton would grow out toward it. Each step took him further from the hub of the town's activity. There were fewer people to shoulder around and the way grew darker; but before the locked door of a feed stable a man lounged. He was taking his ease here, yet there was a strained alertness to him, as though all his faculties were bent upon the three saloons. He said softly, "Good evening, Ballard."

In the first moment he was only a shapelessness in black, with the white of a waistcoat glimmering softly. But he had a cigar in his face, and when he pulled upon it his sensuous features stood sharply revealed. Dan said, "Good evening, Price."

"A hot time in the old town tonight," Price observed.

"It's got the makings," Dan admitted. "I'm on my way to see Potter. Is there any county law in town?"

Another drag at the cigar revealed Price's half-smile. "Not any more, Ballard. The sheriff used to keep a deputy here, but the fellow only grew fat. A couple of years ago the sheriff decided that Potter could handle anything that happened. Now a deputy comes only when he's sent for."

"I was thinking," Dan said, "that Fanshawe could be moved to the county seat. At least until this blows over."

Price said, "I'm surprised at your interest. When I first spotted you just now, I supposed you'd come in to see Cynthia. She's still pretty shaken. What's Fanshawe one way or the other?"

"I wonder," Dan said.

73

Ransome Price tossed the cigar away, and his face was lost now in shadow. He said, "Probably it will all blow over anyway. They'll drink and they'll talk, and some will drink too much and fall on their faces. People as a whole are a pack of fools."

"I wonder," Dan said again.

He brushed on by, wanting no more of this kind of talk. He knew that ever since his return to the range the sight of Ransome Price had stirred an animosity in him. There was something now in the calloused indifference of Price that whetted that animosity. Or was that merely a cloak to cover another feeling that had grown out of the man's constant attentiveness to Cynthia? *You're jealous, you fool!* Dan thought, and was angry with himself.

The jail building shaped ahead. Logs, hauled from the hills, made its foundation, and the superstructure was frame. It was a long, low building with an office to the front, and a lamp burned in the office. The barred cell windows were so many blank eyes. This building often stood empty; its commodiousness was the planning of an earlier day. Four steps led up to the office door. Before the door was a small platform, and here a man could make his stand when the mob came spilling up the street. He'd be above his listeners, Dan observed, and there was an advantage in this, remembered from a public speaking class he'd attended. He had to smile now; the instructor had said nothing about stopping lynch mobs.

He mounted the steps and turned about, facing back toward the street and listening to that muted roar. His thought then was stark and disconcerting. Suppose they were only using the insult to a Ballard as an excuse for all the madness that was in them? Suppose that when he tried to stop them he was only a man who was in their way? He remembered Gramp Ballard saying that a man hadn't lived who hadn't loved and hated and found a cause that was more important than his life. Here, then, was the cause, but there was nothing in it to inspire martyrdom. He didn't want to die that Lew Fanshawe might live. Ransome Price had been right about one thing — Fanshawe wasn't much one way or the other.

Yet there was no turning back now. A man might think his thoughts, yet he couldn't go drifting off into the shadows, putting his back to this thing. Not now. Today he'd had no choice but to fight Fanshawe; tonight, by that same queer inevitability, he had no choice but to defend the man. There was no explaining it; the books had had nothing to say on this subject.

So thinking, he set his hand to the door

and pushed it inward and entered Abe Potter's office.

He remembered the office; it had been the same under a half-dozen town marshals, and he had known it from his childhood. His father had fetched him here once, and there'd been that same spur-scarred, cigarette-burned desk centering the room, the same swivel chair and battered filing case, and possibly the same fly-specked, time-yellowed reward dodgers mottling the wall. But there was this difference: Abe Potter hadn't been stretched upon the floor, a big and ungainly shape with the consciousness gone out of him.

The door to the back of the room, the door giving into the cell corridor, was slightly ajar. Dan crossed the office in a bound; whoever had done this damage to Potter was back there in the corridor, and when he entered its gloomy length, lighted only by a single over-hanging kerosene lamp, he saw the figure at the door of the one occupied cell, the figure who fumbled with Potter's key ring. And seeing her was like a heavy blow, for he had never seen her before but he knew her.

"She's nineteen," Clayton Allison had said. "Usually she wears Levis and a shirt, and she might pass for a boy, but only at a distance. Her hair is black and hangs to her shoulders. Her eyes are black. She's pretty — as pretty as the devil's daughter would be if he had one."

But the words had been too meager; they didn't account for the perfection of April Allison's features, or for something less tangible that struck a man upon seeing her. Hers was a primitive wildness, the wildness of the fawn caught unawares, the wildness of high hills, of singing pine and unfettered stream. She looked at him with her lips slightly parted, her breasts heaving; she looked at him as a trapped beast might have looked.

She would turn and run; he was sure of that. But she didn't run. She fumbled the harder with the keys as he came bearing down upon her. She was here to free Fanshawe, to save him from the mob, but he didn't want Fanshawe saved in this manner, to ride away free as the wind. Dan reached the door and grasped at her, trying to pull her away from the lock, but she'd freed the door and it swung open. Fanshawe had stood close to the bars, encouraging her, probably; he came charging out. His fist swung wildly at Dan and caught him on the chin.

This, then, was Dan's meeting with April Allison, his first meeting and his first parting. He had the picture of her, her eyes startlingly wide, to carry with him as his knees gave away and he went down to the blackness of oblivion.

6

Man and Maiden

He struggled up toward consciousness like a man climbing from the blackness of a well. He became aware of light — sharp, yellow light which beat against his eyeballs and hurt them — but that was much later, after an infinity of shadows. Then he heard voices and movement; these were intangible things that swirled around him and yet remained remote from him. The only reality was pain, a steady soreness of jaw and ribs, and his head throbbed ceaselessly. There was something wrong about his ribs hurting; he knew that, but it took forever to grasp why that was wrong. He guessed then that Fanshawe had kicked him — kicked him after Dan had been knocked down. He used that thought as a man might use a rope, pulling himself upward, and he opened his eyes and saw faces.

He raised a hand to shade his eyes, and Doc Church said, "Take it easy, Dan. Just take it easy."

He was stretched upon the horsehair sofa where Cynthia had lain this afternoon, but it was the medicinal smell of Doc Church's office that first identified the place. From where he lay he could see Church's framed diploma. Time had yellowed the certificate, and the glass was fly-specked, and the frame hung slightly awry. He had an urge to get to his feet and cross the room and straighten that frame; it seemed a most important and necessary thing to do. He got himself upon one elbow, but the pain beat through him with the effort and he gave it up.

Barney Partridge moved into his range of vision and said, "How you feeling, boy?"

"Done in," Dan said. "What a wallop!"

Cynthia was here; she stood looking down upon him, her face strained, her eyes somber. Ransome Price was here, too; he leaned against Church's desk and kept a proper look of sympathy upon his face, but Dan wondered irritably if the man went with the furniture, or what. Abe Potter sat in the swivel chair, his fat face gray, his chin cupped in his hands. Dan knew how Potter felt. Potter had got it, too, and his head was probably beating like a tom-tom.

Doc Church said, "Don't talk unless you feel like it, Dan. But we're all hoping you know more than Abe knows. Somebody sneaked up and got him from behind; he never even had a glimpse of who hit him. The sign says someone fetched two horses into the weeds beside the jail. Fanshawe and the other party took off on those two horses. One of the cayuses was stolen; it was a Tomahawk mount that Mace Cantrell had left in front of the Palace. The old man is frothing."

Remembrance came back to Dan now with a rush — the marshal's office, the heaped body upon the floor, the girl in the corridor, the swung fist of Lew Fanshawe. He tried rising again, and this time got himself to a sitting position. He said, "How much start has Fanshawe got?"

Partridge shook his head. "Hard telling. Enough to clear town, anyway. It was me found you, Dan. I came up to the jail to tell you that it looked like the boys were ready to start marching. How long you'd been knocked out then I wouldn't know. Might have been twenty minutes. Abe was just coming alive."

Potter said, "The last I remember is that I was just going back into the corridor to have a look at Fanshawe. I was nervous as a cat with that mob talking itself into trouble down the street. I had my back to the front door when I got it. Whoever clouted me must walk quiet as a shadow."

Dan brought his fingers to his chin; there was a welt. He said, "I can't tell you much. I walked into the office and found Abe on the floor. That stampeded me a little, I guess.

I dragged open the door leading to the corridor and ran smack into Fanshawe. He used his fist on me. It was a lucky punch; he only had to hit me once."

"Someone must have been with him," Potter said. His broad face knotted with the working of his thoughts. "The party who clouted me got the keys. They were on my desk when the lights went out for me, and they were in the cell door afterwards. Did you only see Fanshawe in the corridor?"

"If there was someone else, he must have been behind Fanshawe. Everything happened so quickly. All I really remember is that fist coming at me."

Ransome Price said, "That's strange. Potter, didn't you say you found the gun lying near Fanshawe's cell door?"

"Here it is," Potter said, and dragged a Colt's forty-five from his belt. "Yours, Dan?"

"Mine," Dan admitted. "Fanshawe must have dragged it from my holster and thrown it back along the corridor so that if I came out of it in a minute I wouldn't be able to lay my hands on a gun." Damn the gun! Probably it had fallen from his holster as he went down. And damn Price's quick way of putting the pieces together! Afraid of what his face might be showing, Dan said, "What about the mob?"

"Some piled onto horses and lit out," Price said. "They'll ride around in circles for a while, trying to cut sign on Fanshawe and his partner, and then they'll give up. Most of them are still here in town, talking it over. They lost the victim for their little blood-letting party, so they've lost their enthusiasm. I told you, Ballard, that they were a pack of fools. "

Potter wagged his great head. "It's beyond town law now. It's work for a deputy from the county seat."

Price's eyes lingered on Dan's face. The gaze held and became steady and compelling, and built an anger in Dan which he knew he mustn't show. He closed his eyes again; he had to do that or lower his gaze, and he asked himself why he'd lied. He remembered the girl vividly, that trapped wildling in the corridor, but he also remembered Clayton Allison and his visit to the Hourglass. He recalled the cynicism of the man, his open contempt for his own daughter. He thought, *I've got to play this out in my own way,* and tried to find an excuse for himself in the thought. But he knew the truth went deeper than that. He knew that some instinct had held him from delivering her name to the law, and because he couldn't name the instinct, his conscience smote him.

He opened his eyes again and returned Price's unblinking stare. He swung his legs around and planted his feet upon the floor and came to a stand. For a moment the room revolved; the faces were a swirling blend, and then he took a tottering step and another and got command of himself. He lifted the gun from Potter's lax fingers and dumped it into the holster. He said, "I may need this. Unless the law has claim on it for evidence."

Potter said, "Fanshawe helped himself to his own guns from my desk before he lit out. A man like him wouldn't want any gun but his own. Likely he lifted your gun to play safe, just as you said."

That gave Dan a bad moment. Potter believed him because he was a Ballard, and a Ballard wouldn't lie. Not to the law. His anger rose against April Allison, a strange, formless anger that was in reality an anger with himself. The little tart! She was in love with Fanshawe, of course.

Cynthia said with genuine concern, "Dan, are you sure you're all right?"

"A night's sleep is what I need." He looked at her; she was steadiness and dependability; she was an arm upon which a man could lean. He said, "I meant to ride to town tonight to talk to you. This lynch business threw me off the track. If you're going home, I'll see you to the cottage."

"I'm going home, Dan," she said.

Dan looked at Price but spoke to Potter. "Anything else tonight, Abe?"

"Reckon not," Potter said. "We both drew blanks, I guess."

Barney Partridge said, "I'll hang around till you're ready to ride out, Dan."

Cynthia took Dan's arm. He crossed from office to anteroom with her and paused in the doorway and bade the others a good night. He opened the door leading to the covered stairway and preceded her down the steps. Sometimes a drunk picked this pocket of darkness in which to do his sleeping. Upon the boardwalk, they strolled in silence; the night air was kind to him, it caressed his face and dulled the throbbing in his head. The hitch-rails seemed less crowded; the mumble still rose from the saloons, but it had a different note to it. Before the Palace he ran his eyes over the standing horses. There were several brands but the Tomahawk was no longer one of them. He found himself smiling. The little vixen! She'd had to steal a horse in order to get Fanshawe away once she'd freed him. But a Tomahawk horse! The nerve of her!

Cynthia sighed. "I'm tired, Dan," she said. "It's been too much for one day."

He groped for her hand and squeezed it;

he was still thinking of April Allison.

Beyond the busier part of town the buildings thinned out; here were the better residences, and the cottage of Doc Church was one of them. It was small and white, and a picket fence surrounded it, and near the gate stood a giant cottonwood, older than the memory of the oldest man. The cottage was Eastern respectability transplanted; it was Doc Church and his daughter portrayed in frame and paint. Dan and Cynthia came silently to the gate and paused here. Starshine trickled through the cottonwood's shivering leaves and laid a lacy pattern upon her face. An awkwardness came between them in this moment; each stood waiting for the other to speak; and Dan said then, "How about it, Cyn?"

"About what, Dan?"

"'You and I."

She lowered her eyes, saying nothing, and he watched and waited and felt the breech widen between them and considered this phenomenon with an odd detachment, as though it concerned someone else who was a stranger to him. She said at last, "About the wedding you mean, I suppose. Don't you think it best that we keep on postponing it? At least till this trouble is over?"

"If that's the way you want it, Cyn."

She drew in a deep breath. "Dan, you've

changed! Oh, I expected you'd be different after three years at school, but the *way* you've changed is what startles me. That gunfight today, and then the fight in the jailhouse tonight. Oh, I know both those things were forced upon you. I've lived too long in this land not to know that a man can't very well sidestep a fight. But it seems that you've become some sort of magnet that attracts violence. That's a little hard to get used to, Dan. Can't you understand?"

"I was your fiancé when I went away," he said. "I'm a stranger now. Is that it?"

She said, "Maybe I've just got to get used to you again. But it can't be done in a day. Or perhaps I'm the one who's changed. I don't know. Things don't look the same to me anymore. I used to love this land; I used to watch for the first wild flowers and see the changing seasons and wonder why all the artists in the world didn't hurry here to paint our prairie. Now even the land looks savage; it almost reaches out to claw at me. If only it would rain!"

He said aghast, "Cynthia! The drought hasn't turned *you* crazy, too?"

"Call it that, if you wish," she said.

He put a long moment's reflection on all this, but it seemed hard to keep his mind at the task. He was tired, he decided, very tired.

He said, "Once we were a couple of people who met and liked each other so much that the liking grew into something stronger. Couldn't we start all over, Cyn? I'll try reaching out for you again. I hope you'll try, too. How about that?"

But even as he spoke, he sensed that this was merely a forlorn hope wrapped in adequate words. Old Man Cantrell was another who hoped to turn back the clock, and Old Man Cantrell would fail because time moved only forward. Yet he wanted this last hold on what there had been between himself and Cynthia, and the tension held in him until she said, "It's a good bargain, Dan. And — and I'll try."

She put her hand to the gate, and he wondered if he was to be permitted to kiss her good night. That wouldn't be going back to the furthest yesterday as he'd just proposed, but he made the try, his arms enfolding her. She lifted her lips, and they were as cool as he'd remembered them, but the surrender had no sweetness in it. It was the kiss a dozen close friends would have gotten afterward, if there'd been a wedding today.

"Good night, Cyn," he said.

When he went back up the street to where he'd left his horse, Partridge moved out of the shadow of a building and stepped up into saddle at the same time. They wordlessly wheeled their mounts and picked their way along the street. When they were upon the prairie and the night had pocketed them, they lifted their mounts to a trot, but this jogging motion seemed to drive Dan's spine upward through his aching head. He reined down to a walk, and Partridge did likewise, and the communion of silence stayed between them until they were abreast of the prairie-dog village and the stars were beginning to fade.

Partridge said then, "Ransome Price saw through it quick, didn't he? About you claiming to have fell at one spot while the gun was found at another."

Dan gave him a sharp glance. "And you know better, eh?"

"It was me found you in the jail, remember? By the cell door, Dan. I dragged you out as far as the office, then decided I'd better go get Doc Church."

Dan stiffened with sudden understanding. He'd been stupid, he decided angrily. He'd even forgotten how to think. Naturally, Barney had known the truth! Known it all the time!

He said, "Thanks for keeping shut."

Partridge shrugged. "Nobody asked me any questions. They were all too excited. Except Price. He helped tote you to Doc's office.

When you spilled your piece, all I had to do to back it was keep my mouth shut."

Here was a man loyal to his salt, and Dan said, "You've got the truth coming to you, Barney."

"I got nothing coming that you don't feel like shelling out."

"You know the Allison girl — the daughter of the fellow who took over Sam Digby's place?"

"I've seen her a time or two when I was riding fence," Partridge said. "Wild as a hawk."

Partridge had seen her, which was more than Wayne had, Dan reflected. Wayne hadn't even known Allison had a daughter. But at least one man on the Hourglass hadn't been completely blind!

"She's the one who sprung Fanshawe out of jail," Dan said.

Partridge gave this silent consideration. Then, "You figger Abe Potter wouldn't be interested to know that?" he asked pointedly.

Dan said, "I know where I'll find Fanshawe. Somewhere around the Allison place. I'm taking that trail tomorrow. I want Fanshawe before the law lays hands on him again. I want to wring the truth out of him. Maybe then I'll quit being the kind of magnet that attracts violence. If I'd talked up tonight, half the town would be riding toward Allison's right now."

Partridge said, "I savvy what you mean."

Did he? Dan wondered if he savvied himself. He'd told a pat story and Partridge had believed it because Partridge was like all the rest — he'd never doubt a Ballard. But Dan could have told the truth to Potter and Doc and Price and asked them to keep it from the rest of the town, and they would have.

He looked out across the night, looked to the north where the hills hemmed the horizon, looked and tried to penetrate the darkness and the distance, knowing that somewhere yonder Lew Fanshawe and April Allison rode stirrup to stirrup. He had lied for the girl, and he couldn't deny it. A man might be dishonest with Abe Potter, but he couldn't be dishonest with himself.

Tomorrow he'd take the trail.

7

The Purgatory

In mid-morning he stood in the ranch yard, his horse saddled and ready to ride, and while he shaped up a cigarette and took his time at smoking it, he let his mind check the preparations he'd made, testing them for adequacy. He might have slept longer, he reasoned. The bed had been hard to leave, but habit had clamored louder than any alarm clock. He had donned range garb, helping himself indiscriminately to whatever was his or Wayne's. He had strapped the gun belt around his middle, placed a pair of binoculars in the saddlebag, debated about toting a rifle and decided against it. The question of a pack horse had required the greatest consideration. He might be in the hills many days; he might finish out his search before the sun went down. He had decided to travel light. Charley had prepared food for the saddlebag, and that would do him, that and the saddle blanket.

The horse stood in the shade of the cook-shack. Already the day's heat had an accumulated intensity, and saddle leather would quickly grow too hot to touch. The crew, coming home sometime during the night and up at the crack of dawn, was gone about its business; Barney Partridge was gone with the others. The ranch seemed to slumber; the clatter of dishes in the cook-shack was the only living thing; the horses stood listlessly in the corral, and the dogs were sleeping somewhere. Dan carefully put out the cigarette, setting his heel upon it and grinding.

Wayne came across the yard, taking his time. He said, "Riding, kid?"

"Just to look over the country."

"Back for supper?"

"Likely."

"You'll make it before midnight?" Wayne insisted, and looked to the north.

"Cantrell's deadline, eh?" Dan said. He'd completely forgotten it.

"If you're riding that direction, you could drop in at the Tomahawk."

"And speak for both of us?"

Wayne shrugged; it was a gesture of tired futility. "I'm sick of thinking about it. Whatever you want to tell the old man will be okay with me."

I'll make the decision, eh? Dan thought. *And if it's against Cantrell and means war, then Barney Partridge will lead the Hourglass in the fighting. You're too sick for that, too. Wayne? Gramp was right. We talked of a better breed of cattle, but what this range needs is a better breed of men. Wayne, what's done this to you? The drought?*

"I'm riding north," Dan admitted. "But I'll not be going to the Tomahawk, Wayne. Not for that, anyway. The day hasn't yet come when the Ballards ride to the Cantrells. Let the Tomahawk come to us for the answer. I'll try to be back by midnight."

Wayne said, "I don't like your riding alone, Dan."

Dan said, "I guess I've been doing it for a long time, Wayne."

He stepped up into the saddle and lifted his hand in salute and sent the horse across the yard in a walk. He looked back once; Wayne was slowly heading toward the house. Someone called, *"Dan!"* but it wasn't Wayne. Dan raised his eyes. Gramp's head sprouted from the upstairs window of his room; the old man beckoned, and Dan wheeled his horse and brought it to the shady side of the gallery and dropped the reins.

He came into the house. At first it seemed so cool here that it was reinvigorating just to be inside; before he'd ascended the stairs he knew this was only an illusion. When he stood framed in the open doorway of Gramp's room, the old man was in his chair, the blanket about his knees, the cane beside him. Dan wondered how Gramp could stand the blanket in this weather. He grinned and said, "Another caning, Gramp?"

"Not that you haven't got it coming," Gramp said testily. "What's this about your gunfighting in the streets like some common rowdy?"

Now how had Gramp known that? He wasn't talking to Wayne these days. Then Dan remembered Barney Partridge.

"I was pushed, Gramp," he said. "I pushed back. I'm not proud of it."

The old man's face was uncompromising; he had bluffed his way through a thousand poker games in his time, had Gramp. He said, "Fanshawe was on the porch of the Rialto. You backed across the street to the far boardwalk. When it was over, they toted Fanshawe to jail, and Doc Church came and put a patch on his shoulder. You didn't do much more than break his skin and shock him. At that distance you should have drilled him plumb center. You're a hell of a tribute to my teaching, Dan!"

"I tilted my gun at the last moment. I didn't want him dead."

A storm gathered in Gramp's eyes. "Have you no brains at all? You humbled a man like him but you left him alive. Don't you savvy that he'll have no rest till he sees you in his gunsight? You had your chance to finish him and you played the fool!"

Dan's lips drew tight and he said, "When I leave a dead man behind me I want to feel in my bones that he deserved to die."

The gathering fury faded from Gramp's eyes; his glance softened and his voice softened. "I could only teach you how to handle a gun," he said. "The rest you had to learn for yourself. But some have to notch their guns and have a parade of dead men between them and their sleep before they learn that there's a place for mercy, even in a gunfighter's code."

His eyes turned bleak again. "You were riding north when I called you back. On your way to knuckle under to the Cantrells?"

"To hell with you, Gramp," Dan said softly.

The old man grinned, but only briefly. "Your wedding's postponed. Decided not to marry her after all?"

"I'll marry her when this trouble is over."

"Bah!" Gramp said, and scowled. "If you loved her, you'd have picked her up in your arms and toted her back to the church, if there wasn't any other way of getting her there. I built too much hope on what happened between you and Fanshawe. You still ain't alive, Dan. It's like you said, you got pushed and you pushed back. A coyote would show that kind of guts. Nothing's changed."

"I wonder," Dan said.

"Git on your way," Gramp said brusquely. "Leave an old man to his miseries. What good's thinking, if you can only think for a fellow like Lew Fanshawe?"

"I found one of those three things you mentioned, Gramp," Dan said. "I found a cause."

"Bah!" Gramp said again. "Would you know if it bit you? Git on your way."

The one step still creaked when Dan came downstairs; it had creaked last night when he'd come in so late; Gramp had stirred in his room. Wayne was somewhere in the house when Dan reached the lower floor; he could hear Wayne prowling about. He went wordlessly to the gallery, climbed the railing and dropped into the saddle, and he didn't look behind him this time as he headed out of the yard.

To the north the prairie was the same unbroken expanse of sage such as lay between Ballardton and the Hourglass except that the land had a more noticeable tilt to it. Coulees and ridges dipped and rose to form a barrier for him as the miles fell behind.

The heat was a steady hammer. Dan's shirt grew sticky between the shoulder blades and his sweat became a stench in his nostrils. He was surprised to find that he was not as stiff as he'd expected to be. He let the horse choose its own gait; he rode loose in the saddle, sparing himself, and even-balanced, sparing the mount. He kept his sombrero brim low enough to shade his eyes; the reflection of sunlight upon the metal trimmings of the bridle was blinding when it struck him. He rode slowly, sometimes not even thinking; he liked this aloneness. Sometimes he dozed.

In early afternoon he came to Ballard Springs. He had seen the sunlight reflecting from the barbed wire across the last long miles; drawing closer, he'd made out the movement of cattle around that wire, and the figure of a man. It was an Hourglass rider; Dan recognized him as he rode up. He was called Pete, and if he had a last name to go with it he had kept it to himself. He was one of the older hands and he greeted Dan with no show of surprise and only the shadow of a grin to indicate any appreciation for company on a long and lonely vigil.

"I handle the gate," he said, indicating the fence with a jerk of his thumb. "We water so many a day — share and share alike. But I reckon you know that."

The cattle gathered around the fence wore the Hourglass brand. They bawled piteously, steadily, smelling the water and thirsting for it, and a man had to raise his voice above their discordance. Pete said, "Let 'em in and they'd bloat themselves; haze 'em away and they only drift back. It's plain hell, ain't it?"

Dan said, "It's plain hell."

He looked at the water bubbling up out of the ground; the spring seemed smaller than he'd remembered it. Around the edges was caked earth, mud dried hard in the sun and dented by many hoofprints. He dismounted and crawled through the wire and stretched himself prone and sucked in the water; it had a good, clean taste; there'd been no water like this in the East. He let his horse through the gate, loosened the cinch, let the animal drink a little, pulled it back from the water with an effort, then let it drink a little more. He came through the fence again and mounted; he sat his saddle looking upon the water, looking upon the miracle of it. Five of these with the proper piping, and this range would be a garden!

He said, "Got to be riding. So long, Pete."

Beyond the springs the country lifted out of its flatness; now the foothills of the Rimfires spread before him and an occasional tree stood stark and lonely. The sun grew pitiless; heat ran its shimmering waves over the land; and a jack rabbit, bounding from a sage clump and jumping away, seemed to be disembodied, floating in the haze, losing itself to Dan's sight. He got his gun out when he saw the rabbit;

he had the gun tilted when he thought better of the act and restored the weapon to its holster. He thought, *You and Fanshawe — you and Fanshawe, Jack* — but still there was no real regret in him.

He became aware of hunger and ate, never leaving the saddle. The way lifted ever upward; he found himself upon a promontory and rested his horse here. Below him the range spread to the eye's limit; he could see Ballardton, a fairy town, seemingly suspended in the distance. Nearer was the Hourglass — he could pick out each building and put a name to it — and nearer yet the sunlight caught the glint of Ballard Springs and made it a bit of diamond in the drab, burned setting. He sought and identified the Circle-Bar, the Hashknife, and the Wagon Wheel; all three spreads lay to the west of the Hourglass. Behind him the hills reared; they had promised coolness from the distance, but there was no coolness.

He remembered Gramp Ballard; Gramp had first found his way to the range here at its north end; he had sought a pass through the Rimfires and spilled a few thousand longhorns down into the lush graze. He tried seeing this land as Gramp had seen it that long-gone day; he erased the town and the ranches from the picture and gave a greenness to the prairie in his mind's eye, and he was Gramp, sitting a saddle and looking upon trail's end.

Gramp had been alone, and here was what he'd been seeking. At first there'd been only Gramp, and then the Cantrells had come and holed up in the hills. Was that what made a Ballard a Ballard — being first? But Dan knew there was more to it than that, and more to it than owning the springs and having all the neighbors beholden. He knew that leadership had been made of something that bore no name, something that a man was born to or never achieved, something that could be dying; and he knew now why Gramp sat in his chair from day to day brooding, and bedded each night with bitterness.

He wheeled the horse and rode on; it was not until he was climbing again that he sensed that he was running from the thoughts he'd had on the promontory. Presently he came out upon the rim of a gorge and looked down upon the Purgatory, that most useless of rivers. The high hills yonder gave birth to the Purgatory, sired among the peaks and lunging downward, wild and tumultuous. Across the span of the ages it had cut itself a deep canyon which narrowed to a long impassable gorge at this point, and here the rapids thundered eternally. As a boy, Dan had heard that tumult; it had held a sinister note; it was a giant running rampant down a mountainside. Now it spoke of other things, of wasted water, of what might have been a solution to all problems, a solution that was ever-present but just out of reach. Though the canyon widened below, it remained always a scar across the length of the range; there were very few places where its walls were not too precipitous to allow the watering of cattle. Far to the south, on another range, the Purgatory gave life to a thirsty land. Here it was nothing — nothing but a clamor and a defeat.

Riding along the rim, Dan dismounted and walked out upon an overhanging rock which thrust outward like a thumb over the edge of the near wall. A hundred feet down lay a deep pool, just below the brawling, white-capped stretch of rapids through the upper canyon. Dan stretched himself out upon the rock; the heat of it bit through his shirt and made him wince. He looked downward; the Purgatory was shallower than he'd ever remembered it; he could see ledges of rock below that had been submerged in other seasons. And he saw the man who worked his way along one of the ledges.

At first Dan knew stark terror. Was the fool trying to kill himself? He could think of no reason in the name of sanity why a man should have descended to the bottom of the gorge.

101

Yonder, flat against the face of the near wall, he saw the means by which the descent had been made — a knotted rope anchored to a stunted tree that grew on the lip of the gorge. He peered again at the man; there was no identifying him. He remembered the binoculars; he went back to the horse and got the glasses from the saddlebag and stretched himself out again and had a look. Now the man leaped at his vision; he was tall and thin and angular, but oddly it was the crisscrossing suspenders that identified him to Dan, for the man was stooped, feeling his way along the ledge with his back to Dan. He was Clayton Allison. Now what was Allison doing on Hourglass land, Dan wondered. And why had he worked his way down there?

He tried adjusting the glasses for better vision. He worked at them and at last got Allison into clear focus. The man had straightened up; he stood peering about, and he was holding a torpedo-shaped instrument that appeared to be about two feet long. He edged around a bend in the ledge and was momentarily lost to sight. When he showed himself again, he had managed to clamber down to the water's edge. From above, it looked as though the water lapped hard against the canyon's walls. It was obvious now that this was not so, at least in this dry year with the river down. The man vanished around another turn.

Pulling himself to a stand and backing from the rim, Dan restored the binoculars to the saddlebag and mounted. There was something about that torpedo-shaped instrument that tugged at his memory, but he had ridden a half mile before the recollection blossomed into fullness. He remembered college and a man he'd roomed with his second year, and a friend of his roommate, a redheaded fellow. That redhead had been an engineering student. And he'd had one of those instruments. Dan had examined the thing once and asked what it was. A current meter, used in making hydrographic surveys.

The horse balked; it had grown increasingly skittish ever since they'd started paralleling the gorge's rim. Dan fought its fractiousness absently, his hand at the task, his mind elsewhere.

8

Digby's Place

Now the north line of the Hourglass was behind him and he was toiling up Tomahawk Pass. Once this had been a game trail, no more than that. Usage and crude engineering had widened it to a wagon road, but it was a poor sort of road, for the passage of many cattle had crumbled the ruts. The Cantrells spilled their beef down this ancient highway every fall to trail them south to the shipping pens at Ballardton, and even at this season there were signs of recent movement. Cattle fetched down to Ballard Springs to share the water with the others, Dan decided. The pass was a giant stairway with levels and steep pitches and not as many switchbacks as a man might expect. It was an avenue open to all; this stretch of it was on Sam Digby's holdings; above lay the Tomahawk ranch. Now Clayton Allison owned the land upon which Dan rode.

Allison, who was at the bottom of Purgatory Gorge with a current meter in his hands.

Timber stood thick to the left of the trail; lodgepole pine built a solid barrier that would permit only of erratic passage. Dan had looked to the trees with longing the last miles; they kept the sun from him now, but the heat seemed more intensified; the woods had a tinder-dry smell to them and a tinder-dry look to them. It was a wonder there hadn't been forest fires this season. He began being very careful about his smoking and to space his cigarettes further apart. The tobacco was dry and tasteless today; it gave him little comfort. Needles paved the trail, but this did not make the slippery, spongy underfooting he remembered. Once, dismounting, he scooped up a handful of them and felt their brittleness and shook his head. Within an hour he crossed two creek beds, one bone dry, and one with a mere thread of water.

He left the trail a few miles above the gorge, where a road had been cleared through the timber. He knew this road; it had cost Sam Digby many weeks of labor. Back in here was the old Digby place, and the timber gave way to small meadows and grassy coulees where beef could thrive. Digby had never been a large operator; he had made a poor man's living and seemingly been satisfied with it, and it had been something of a surprise when he'd sold out to Allison. Ransome Price would likely know the ins and outs of that. Price had handled the sale — or so Wayne had once written.

The buildings that lay ahead were still

105

screened from the eye, but Dan knew that any moment now he would burst upon them. He had become a manhunter since leaving the pass trail, yet he rode with no attempts at silence; he rode as a man would ride who is making a call upon a neighbor. That was why he'd decided against the rifle. He had based this trip upon a theory that April Allison would have brought Lew Fanshawe to the hills, but he had not forgotten the contemptuous references Clayton Allison had made concerning his daughter the night before. They were enemies, those two, father and daughter, and April wouldn't dare bring Fanshawe to the place. But she would hide him out somewhere near here. She would need food for him and perhaps medicine — there was that bullet wound — and thus the old Digby place would be the hub from which any real search should be made.

And Clayton Allison was away from the ranch. Here was the perfect time for April to be stealing food for the man she was hiding.

So thinking, Dan rode into a stump-mottled clearing and reined up before a sagging, peeled-pole fence that enclosed a log house sprawled aimlessly in the center of the yard. Scattered about were various outhouses, all of them made of logs, all of them looking in need of repairs. Sam Digby had had a greater pride in appearance than the new owner. A few chickens scratched disconsolately in the clearing. Flies droned about; the lowering sun beat down.

Dan dismounted and let the reins drop. He came through an opening in the fence and crossed the sagging porch of the house and rapped smartly upon the door. The droning silence held. He had expected no answer; he had expected instead a soft scurrying, a furtive betrayal if April were alone inside. Frowning, he moved along the porch until he stood before a window. When he first tried peering he could see nothing; he ventured nearer and finally leaned toward the glass, placing his hands to the sides of his face and shielding his eyes. The living room into which he looked still held Sam Digby's homemade furniture; it had gone with the place. He came down off the porch and led his horse into the yard to the pump; he worked the creaky mechanism until the trough was a few inches full. He let the mount drink, then put his mouth under the pump and slaked his own thirst.

Pulling the horse away from the trough, he looped the reins around the top bar of the fence. He walked toward the barn; its door was open, and he strode into the dark interior and paused here. He had the feeling of being watched; it grew upon him until his shoulder blades tingled. A ladder led to a loft. Would she have dared to bring Fanshawe here? He climbed the ladder as silently as he could, but it creaked beneath his weight. He poked his head carefully through the opening; the loft was empty, it would be another week or two before haying began. He came back down the ladder and stepped out of the barn.

Around this place the timber pressed; across the brassy vault of sky overhead a hawk wheeled. A man out there with a rifle, or even a six-shooter, could pick him off like a clay pigeon in a shooting gallery, he realized. He grew suddenly sick of this furtive gumshoeing. He crossed back to the house boldly and put his hand to the door. It gave to his touch and he shouldered inside and closed the door behind him.

The room held a musty, stifling hotness. There was a center table, a few crude chairs, some strips of faded carpet upon the bare boards of the floor. A map lay spread upon the table, its corners held down by rocks. Upon one wall a fly-specked calendar three years old was tacked. A few books stood upon a shelf on another wall. For a long moment Dan stood listening. He said, "Hello —" cautiously, and got no answer. He crossed the room; a faded curtain hung in a doorway, and he swept this aside. Beyond was a bedroom that had been Sam Digby's. Now it was April's, Dan judged; the wall was covered with pictures clipped from magazines and pinned there. He looked at these; three were of stage actors of international fame; the rest were city scenes — carriages on Broadway, Delmonico's restaurant, women promenading in fashionable clothes.

Backing from the bedroom, he looked into the kitchen. He saw a rusty range that had been Digby's, a table, cupboards. Beyond the kitchen was a lean-to, also screened by a curtain. In the lean-to was a cot with a tangle of blankets upon it; whoever slept here had not made his bed. Beside the cot was a small stand, and upon it a book lay open. Dan had a look at the book. It dealt with hydraulic engineering. This, then, was where Clayton Allison slept.

Dan came back into the living room and looked closer at the books upon the shelf; these, too, were engineering books. He bent over the map upon the table. It was a topographical map of the upper range, showing Purgatory River and the gorge. Along the margin were notes made in a cramped precise fist, all of them couched in technical language that was just so much gibberish to Dan.

He had his back to the door as he bent over the map. He didn't hear the door open. He only heard Clayton Allison say in that soft, modulated voice of his, "Raise your hands!"

He raised his hands before he turned around. He remembered that sensation of being watched, and he thought. *He knew I was in here. That's why he came cat-footing.* Allison stood loosely in the open doorway; he had a six-shooter in his hand, and his thin, bloodless lips were drawn in a straight line, and his eyes were bleak and cold. Over his left arm he had a lariat coiled. He said, "Turn around again and put your hands behind your back, your wrists together."

Dan said hotly, "Now see here —"

"Turn around!" Allison snapped. "Do you think anybody would hold me to account for shooting down a man I caught breaking into my house?"

Dan obeyed; he felt a loop fitted over his wrists and drawn tight; he felt that rope wrapped again and again. Allison tripped him then, throwing his shoulder against Dan at the same time. Dan went down to the floor and Allison came down upon him, his knee in the small of Dan's back. Dan flailed his legs, not caring now about Allison's gun, but the rope went around his ankles and stopped his wild threshing, and in a moment he was hog-tied. Allison lifted the gun from Dan's holster and laid it carefully upon the table. Dan rolled over on his side and glared at the man. Allison looked at him remotely, neither interested nor disinterested; the man seated himself upon the nearest chair and laid his own gun on the table beside Dan's. He said, "Well, Ballard?"

The man must have just about finished his business in the gorge, Dan concluded. Even so, how had he got back here so quickly? But a man familiar with the lay of the land would have his own shortcuts. Obviously Allison had approached this place from a different direction and seen him from the timber and bided his time, waiting to see what Dan was doing.

Dan said, "You're new to this country, I know. You don't jump a man for walking into your place. That's why doors are left unlocked on this range."

Allison said, "Suppose you tell me what brought you here."

"April," Dan said.

Allison gave this full consideration, his aristocratic face hardening with the run of his thoughts. "Maybe I've got two reasons for shooting you," he said.

"You were looking for her last night. I might have come to find out if you'd found her. A lost girl could be any man's worry."

Allison's lip curled. "That's a poor bluff, Ballard."

Anger needled Dan. "And you're a poor sort

of father, Allison."

"So?" Allison said. "And what would you know about it, Ballard?" He pulled himself from the chair and crossed to the bookshelf and took down one of the engineering books. From its pages he shook a photograph; he fetched this across the room and knelt and held it a few inches before Dan's nose. It was the picture of a woman's face. It might have been April Allison's except that this woman's hair was piled high and there was a petulance about her mouth; it was the mouth of a woman spoiled by a knowledge of her own beauty.

Allison said, "That's her mother. The face of an angel and the heart of a devil. Have you ever considered woman and her place in the world, Ballard? Behind any successful man you'll find a woman — remember Abraham Lincoln's statement about his mother? But what all the mealymouthed philosophers have overlooked is that women are back of all evil, too. Have you ever heard any orator point out that for every man who's failed, there's been a woman who contributed to his failure?"

Dan said, "She was your wife?"

"I told you last night," Allison said, "that my daughter's way with men was an inherited trait. How would you like it, Ballard, if a woman ruined your life and you counted her dead and then saw her born all over again?"

There was a streak of madness in him. That was it! He was insane on this one subject; his wife had put this kink in him, so he hated the daughter. Dan had found the core of Allison's queerness, and there was no comfort in it, no reality to the moment. This was like something from a bad dream, this lying here upon the floor, drenched with his own sweat and trussed up like a hog while a man made mad talk. Allison restored the picture to the book and said then, as though he'd aroused himself from a reverie, "You were away for schooling, Ballard. Just what did you study?"

"What does it matter?" Dan countered.

"It matters a very great deal."

"A lot of things," Dan said.

"Engineering?"

"None of that."

"I was once an engineer," Allison said. "But you've probably guessed as much since you were looking at the map when I opened the door. It's only a hobby now. I'm a gentleman rancher by choice. You've seen my place. There's no use in my telling you that I'm a very inept rancher."

Dan understood then. Here was a man with a secret, a deadly, dangerous secret. Allison didn't know that Dan had seen him at the bottom of the gorge, but he did know that Dan had seen the map. That was why he was worried over whether Dan knew anything about engineering. And that was why Dan was tied up now. If Allison thought he knew too much, then Dan wasn't to ride away from here. Dan had known humiliation and anger in this brief encounter with Allison. Now, for the first time, he tasted fear.

He said, "Look, Allison, I'm not some saddle-bum who broke into your place to steal. I knocked and no one replied. Maybe I had no business coming inside. But you had no business jumping me with a gun. Loosen these ropes and we'll call it quits."

Allison lifted his own gun from the table. For a long moment he stood looking down upon Dan; he said nothing and there was no guessing the run of his thoughts. He turned toward the door, and he looked back then, a genuine regret in those intelligent eyes. He said, "What the devil did you have to come snooping for, Ballard? Now I've got a devil of a choice to make!"

Dan said, "Think twice, man! Don't you suppose I'll be missed?" Strong in him was the feeling that he was arguing for his life. "Do you want all the Hourglass riders swarming up here?"

"I'll be back," Allison said and left the house, closing the door after him.

Dan heard the man's boots beat across the

yard; he thought he heard the jingle of a bit chain, but he couldn't be sure. Had Allison left a horse in the timber? The man had gone riding — but where? And why? When it came down to it, Allison had two choices — to free Dan or to kill him. Why hadn't he done one or the other?

Dan lay waiting an interminable time, not moving, just listening. He became conscious of a clock ticking; it was in April's bedroom, he guessed, though he couldn't remember seeing it when he'd looked in. He struggled with the ropes; it was a waste of effort that brought the sweat down into his eyes. He tried rolling; to do so he had to press his face against the faded carpeting; it smelled of ancient dust, and he almost choked. He could maneuver himself across the room if he wanted to put forth the effort, but what was to be gained by it? He lay still, his heart pounding, and had a look around, trying to find somewhere in the room an article that might be used to free him. There was nothing.

He thought of the kitchen. Surely there'd be a butcher knife out there, and perhaps he could get his hands on it. But it would take a lot of struggling to reach the kitchen. With his heels drawn up almost to his wrists, there was no way of coming to a stand and hobbling along. The westering sun laid a patch of light through the window and upon the floor; he watched this patch crawl and listened to the clock tick and tried to gauge the passage of time. He tired of this and decided to make a try for the kitchen; at least it would give him something to do.

There was enough slack in the rope between his heels and his wrists to allow him to draw his knees up a little farther. He got on his knees and started inching along on them, but it was slow work, and when he tried too hard, he threw himself off balance and fell sideways to the floor. He was angry for a while, and he voiced his anger until he realized the childishness of this. He looked again at the patch of light and decided that Allison had been gone an hour. It had seemed like three. He heard the tread of footsteps upon the porch then, and panic clutched at his throat. He heard the hand at the door, and he knew that in a moment the door would open.

He thought, *He's made up his mind now. One way or the other!* And he thought, too, that this would be a mighty poor way to die, trussed and helpless and not able to lift a hand in his own defense.

9

One Way Out

Ransome Price had breakfasted earlier than usual that morning, and that was significant, for he was a man of meticulous habits. Of the three restaurants in Ballardton he favored Ching Li's; he had at one time and another inspected the kitchens of all three and Ching Li's was the cleanest. Also, Ching Li never badgered him with small and useless talk while he ate; in this establishment he could occupy a solitary table unmolested while the talk of the other patrons went on around him. He'd long ago learned that the man who listens grows wiser than the man who talks.

This morning he took his time with his food; men greeted him as they came through the doorway; two or three crossed to his table and passed the time of day. Price commanded a respect in Ballardton; he had nursed that respect and carefully reared it across the years. It was a stock in trade, worth more to him than admiration or the camaraderie that some men commanded. Price had never consciously cared whether people truly liked him or not.

Breakfast finished, he came to the board-walk. In this golden hour the town lay mellow, some of its harshness softened by the first light; yonder, on the prairie, a meadow lark sang until its music was lost in the creaking of a pump. Price sighed, thinking that the day promised to be hot again, for there was a ride he had to make. He smiled remembering that he wanted it to be hot at the end of that ride. He had been an opportunist all of his days, and this drought was the greatest opportunity he had known. One cloud in the west might spoil everything.

He began pacing the street, as was his custom. He always took a turn up one side and down the other each morning. "Walking off my breakfast," he'd say to anybody who was curious. But this was in reality his way of keeping his fingers on the town's pulse. He made a fine figure as he strode along, a tall man in black, his suit conservatively cut, the heavy gold watch chain the only sign of opulence about him. He was entirely conscious of how he looked against the setting of Ballardton; he had chosen his garb with care, and the watch chain had been a studied afterthought. These things, too, were part of his stock in trade.

Abe Potter lounged before the open doorway of the blacksmith shop. To him Price said, "Good morning, Potter. A bad night last night."

Potter instinctively raised a plump hand to his head. "A helluva night," he agreed.

"Any news of the fugitives?"

"Those that rode out from town rode back," Potter said. "They cut no sign. But most of 'em were so drunk they couldn't have seen a horse track if they'd been drinking out of it. I sent a wire to the county seat about the matter, but a whale of lot of good it will do. After all, Fanshawe was only in for disturbing the peace. County law will think I'm making a mountain out of a molehill."

"Fanshawe's probably heading over the Rimfires," Price said. "This range has seen the last of him."

"I hope so," Potter sighed.

The street, so crowded yesterday, was almost deserted this morning. A few horses stood languidly at hitchrails, a few men moved aimlessly along the boardwalks, their boots beating an echoing cadence in the early hush. Price moved on, but he did not cross over when he came abreast of the last of the business establishments; instead he walked onward to where the buildings thinned out, coming in due course to the cottage of Doc Church. Price looked upon this small, white building with an approving eye. He put his hand to the gate and passed beneath the giant cottonwood and climbed to the porch and rapped upon the door. Getting no answer, he skirted the house and came to the yard behind it and said, "Good morning, Cynthia," taking off his hat and bowing ever so slightly.

The Churches had a garden back here, made possible by diligent hauling of water from the pump, but it was a sorry sort of garden this season. There were some blighted-looking potato plants, a row or two of corn, withered and scrawny, some peas and beans. Cynthia was picking peas; she wore a gingham dress and a sunbonnet to match it. She straightened herself, holding the peas in her apron, and her smile was both warm and wan as she recognized the man.

She said, "Good morning, Ransome," then sighed. "It's going to be another hot one."

He said, "I knocked at the front door."

"Dad's still sleeping. I'm afraid yesterday was a little trying for him."

"And for you," he said, putting a proper amount of sympathy into his voice.

She sighed again. "I'm probably not the first bride who was left waiting at the church, even in Ballardton."

"Ballard rode out last night?" The question went deeper than the words in which it was couched; he was sure she would sense the depth of it.

"We had a talk," she said. "There'll be no

wedding, at least not for a long while. Did he seem different to you, Ransome? Changed, in a hard sort of way?"

He made no answer to these questions. He stood looking at her for a long moment weighing the possibilities of the moment; he stood there with his hat in his hand. He had a high crown of black hair that curled at the temples, and there was just a hint of gray in it. The sun had never given him the leathery hue it gave others, nor had it squinted his eyes. He knew how he must look to her, something civilized in a savage land, a man of means and promise. He said then, "I would never have spoken of this, Cynthia, while you were pledged to him, but I think you've known how I feel about you."

She dropped her eyes, sudden confusion bringing a rush of color to her cheeks. "Yes, Ransome, I've known," she said.

He looked about him; a hedge separated this yard from the next, cutting off the view. They were alone, and he could have stepped forward and put his arms around her. He debated for a moment, wondering if he should, and he decided against it. There was a day for making that ride he had to make, and this was the day. There would be a day for taking her in his arms, but that day hadn't yet come. He said, "I don't expect an answer now, Cynthia.

121

You haven't even been free to think about such a thing. I'll wait. In the meantime, please keep remembering me as your friend, at least. Whenever you need me, call on me. It's only you that's made this town worth staying in."

He left her then, but he paused at the corner of the house and looked back and smiled, making of the smile a warm and intimate thing. She smiled back, and in her smile was half-a-promise. His stride was longer and springier as he headed back toward the busier part of Ballardton.

Before his land and loan office, he fished a key from his pocket and let himself into the little frame building. To the front of this building was his office, a cubicle furnished with a desk and chair and files and a small iron safe; giving from this room was a door leading to his living quarters. He used this office only for the transacting of paper business; most of the work of buying and selling land was done out on the range. He took his mail from the inner pocket of his coat and placed the mail on his desk; he had picked it up at the post office on his way to breakfast and scanned it while eating. He had a daily calendar on his desk; he picked this up and tore off a sheet and looked at the new date, staring at it for a long time. *This is it!* he thought, and his eyes showed his satisfaction.

He stripped off his coat, and from a desk drawer he lifted a shoulder holster and belt with a late model Colt's forty-five. He strapped the weapon under his left armpit and donned the coat again and picked up the *Back Soon* sign from the top of the desk. When he'd let himself out of the office and locked the door, he hung this sign upon the handle. He lifted his hat to Lily Greer, the spinsterish proprietor of the millinery, who was sweeping the boardwalk before her establishment, and he headed up the street to the livery stable which lay between here and the jail.

He had a saddler of his own but no place to stable the mount so he kept it at the livery. It was a buckskin gelding, a big, dependable horse that had carried him countless miles. He had the hostler do the saddling; a man marked himself by whether he did his own menial tasks or left them for the hands of others. He climbed into the saddle and took the alley behind Ching Li's and stopped and picked three empty tin cans from the top of Ching Li's trash barrel and stowed these in his saddlebag.

He followed the wagon road out of Ballardton to the north. The sun was making itself felt before the first sage-dotted miles were behind him; he let the horse choose its own pace and thus kept to a steady, mile-eating gaiting. He stripped off his coat before noon and tied it behind the saddle; he left the road near the prairie-dog village and cut diagonally across the country to where a coulee grooved the terrain. Choke-cherry bushes grew here; in other years there'd been a creek which was only a dry scar of gravel today.

He took the three empty cans from the saddlebag and lined them up upon the ground at the coulee's bottom after dismounting and leading his horse down there. He paced away from the cans, counting his steps. At a distance which satisfied him, he let his arms hang slackly, then raised his right hand, snatched at the gun, spun on his heel with the same motion, and fired. He sent three shots in such quick succession that they might have been one; the sound blended and was a steady roll, and the cans leaped into the air. He walked back to them and had a look, using his thumb to measure the distance from the top of each can to the bullet hole. He nodded, smiling a grim smile. He lined up the cans again, turning them so that an unblemished surface was exposed, and repeated his performance.

He spent over an hour at this, not always shooting but sometimes sitting upon a large rock that had once perched upon the bank of the creek, sitting there and staring at the cans or just drawing the gun and sighting it without firing. He had practiced in this manner on every solitary ride he had taken; he had gained a skill that would have amazed Ballardton's citizenry. This was his secret; and this was his insurance in a land that had presumed its violent days were behind it. To the livery-stable man who had once glimpsed the gun beneath Price's armpit and remarked on it, Price had said, "I carry it in case I run across a rattlesnake." He had smiled then and added, "Do you suppose I could hit one if I were standing over it?"

When he mounted and rode out of the coulee the cans were shapeless and beyond any further use for his purpose, and the supply of bullets he carried in the saddlebag was half depleted.

The sun stood almost at zenith. The land had taken to undulating and there was no breath of air, and he would have given five dollars for a drink of water. He thought about the heat; it was insidious, it was something a man talked about in the morning, just as he might talk about the meal he would eat when he grew hungry, but not really caring about it, not having more than a remote interest. But, like the hunger, the heat grew on a man with the passing hours, it built itself slowly into something almost tangible, something ever present, something clamoring and pitiless.

In early afternoon he reached the caprock rim and paused here, putting on his coat, and then he topped the rim and came down the shale-mottled slant to the Hourglass buildings. The dogs came charging to greet him, their sharp barking bringing Wayne to the gallery. An edginess gripped Wayne; Price saw this instantly. Wayne said, "Oh, it's you," both relieved and disappointed. Then, "Light and rest your saddle. Had dinner?"

"How's a man to work up an appetite in this heat?" Price said as he stepped down. He led the horse to the watering trough and was careful that the mount didn't drink too long. Price himself had a drink from the pump and walked back to the gallery. "Come inside," Wayne said. "It's a little cooler."

They stepped into the big room with the cavernous fireplace; Wayne waved his visitor to one of the chairs and seated himself facing Price. There was an open curiosity in Wayne; he had played the host but all the while he'd been wondering what fetched Price. Seeing this, Price wasted no time with prelude. He said, "I'm out here to ask if you folks would consider selling the Hourglass?"

Wayne said, "Who the devil would buy it?"

"I thought you'd be surprised," Price said.

126

"Everybody wants to sell this season, but nobody wants to buy. Here's a stroke of luck for you. I've had correspondence with a group of Eastern investors. They were looking for a big place with certain qualifications, and the Hourglass fits to a T. They plan on developing a sort of summer resort place for Eastern visitors who'll be paying guests. They want prairie where the guests can go horseback riding. They want hills near by where they can hunt and fish. And here's the funniest thing of all: They were enraptured over my description of Purgatory River. It's the most useless river in creation by anybody's standards — but to them it's scenic. Can you imagine that?"

"How much will they offer?"

"I suggested one hundred thousand dollars. They didn't seem to think it unreasonable."

"A hundred thousand! Good heavens, man, the Hourglass is worth three times that much!"

"In a good year, yes," Price admitted. "But what's the drought doing to this range? And you're counting the cattle; my buyers would be interested only in the land. Besides, there's more to think about than price, if you consider selling."

"I'm not sure I know what you mean."

Price spread his hands in a patient gesture. "Look, Ballard, there's no use of you and I beating around the bush. It's common knowledge that Old Man Cantrell wants a lease on Ballard Springs. It's likewise known that you've got to give him an answer by midnight tonight. The whole range is hanging on your answer. Most of the small outfits are confident that you'll tell him to go chase his tail and that the water will still be available to everyone. But if you buck him, Cantrell isn't going to take it lying down. You're in for trouble. Here's one way out of it. You could sell to my people."

In Wayne now was the birth of a hope; it showed in his eyes, and Ransome Price read the sign, and the moment ran into a lengthy silence that built a singing tension. Then Wayne's shoulders sagged, and the old weariness rode him again, and he said, "I'll have to talk to Dan. He's gone riding today. He's got something to say about this."

"And *I've* got something to say, too!" Gramp Ballard spoke from the doorway.

He stood there, a lean, stooped figure, his weight upon his cane. How he'd negotiated the stairs would be forever a mystery; how long he'd stood listening was something that could only be guessed at. A high anger was in him, and he said, "A hundred thousand dollars, eh! A hundred thousand for the sweat and blood and dreams of three generations of my family! A hundred thousand dollars and the selling out of our neighbors. That's what you're hollering, Price!"

Price came to his feet, donning respect, donning patience. "I'm acting only as an agent for people with a legitimate proposition, sir. Most ranchers in the section are anxious to sell. Their places don't meet the requirements. I thought I was doing this family a favor."

"A favor." Gramp snorted. "When did your money-grabbing breed ever do anybody a favor? You let good men settle the land and leave their scalps to dry in Indian lodges and their bones to bleach on the prairies, and your kind came along when the land was settled and the towns built and fastened onto them like leeches and tried sucking them dry. A parasite is the kindest word I can think of to tag onto you! Now get off Hourglass land and take your stinking proposition with you!"

"Gramp!" Wayne cried, aghast.

Price still stood, the red creeping up from his collar line, but he looked at Wayne and managed a smile. And thus Price, at the moment, was a man insulted, but a man with too much dignity to him to answer the insult in kind; he played this role to perfection. He said, "It seems I'm not wanted here. Good afternoon, gentlemen."

Gramp had turned and limped out of sight.

That one step creaked beneath his weight as he negotiated the stairs again. Price came out upon the gallery, Wayne at his elbow. Wayne said awkwardly, "I don't know what to say. He's an old man, and he's been ailing. We have to put up with his abuse every day. But I didn't think —"

Price smiled and laid a hand upon Wayne's shoulder. "Never mind, Ballard. I understand." He crossed the yard to his horse, Wayne still trailing him. "The proposition's still open," Price said. "And it's still a way out for you. Talk it over with your brother when he comes home."

"Couldn't you stay for supper?" Wayne said helplessly.

"Thanks, no. But I do appreciate this invitation. I don't hold this against *you*, Ballard. Nor against him, really. As you say, he's an old man and ailing."

Price offered his hand; Wayne took it, and Price stepped up to saddle. From the top of the caprock rim he looked back and lifted his hand to Wayne, who still stood in the yard, the sun strong upon him. But once over the rim, the smile died on Price's lips and a cold fury shook him and the horse felt his spurs. He let that anger ride with him for a mile; through his mind ran a steady stream of silent profanity, and then he recovered himself and hauled the horse down to a walk. He had learned patience long ago.

Yet he was still grim of lip when he rode into Ballardton at sundown. He gave no more than a grunt to the hostler's observation that the day had been a scorcher. He went to Ching Li's and ate morosely and came up the street to his office in the gray of twilight. When he let himself into the building, he wished he'd remembered to pull the shades before departing; the little cubicle held all the piled-up heat of the day.

He was sitting at his desk, the lamp unlighted, doing nothing, when he heard the knock at the rear door. It was not a furtive knock, it was loud and insistent and compounded of many things, and a frenzy of impatience was one of them. Price crossed his living quarters and opened the rear door and looked at the man who stood framed there; and surprise put a rigidity in Price and left him wordless for a moment.

Then, "Allison!" he said. "You fool, don't you realize it's not quite dark yet?"

Clayton Allison had the dust of hard riding upon him; it coated his clothes and made him look ghastly. But it was his face that would have held any man's eye. Upon it was the look of a man who had wrestled with the devil across a span of time and space and found no peace. He came into the room quickly and closed the door and put his back to it and fought for breath for a long moment.

Then he said, "I had to risk getting in here without waiting. Things have gone completely wrong, and there's hell to pay. Dan Ballard's up at my place, hog-tied upon the floor. I caught him in my house looking at that damn' map. I can't be sure, but I'm guessing that he knows everything."

"God!" Price ejaculated and fell back a step, and his thought was that this day, the one that had been the most promising of days, had turned sour in every respect.

10

Blindman's Buff

To Dan Ballard it seemed to take forever for the door of the Digby place to open; he had rolled himself over at the first fall of footsteps upon the porch, and he lay now looking at the door. It swung inward and she stood framed there; she made a small and frightened sound in her throat. She hadn't been expecting this, and he supposed she'd scream or faint. She came inside and swung the door shut and stood staring down at him; her eyes were wide and her breasts lifted and thrust hard at the plaid shirt she wore; these were the signs of her astonishment and excitement, these only.

He said, "Don't just stand there! Untie me, can't you?"

She didn't seem to hear him. She said, "Dad did this!"

Incongruously he was thinking that she stood the test of daylight. Her skin was clear and flawless; her eyes darker than her father's. Her lips were slightly parted, her teeth small and white. She was that woman in the photograph, but there was this difference: she was unspoiled. He wondered if this was all she'd ever known, mountains and prairies and other ramshackle places like this. Why had Allison hidden her from the sight and knowledge of men, a child like her? But she was no child; he remembered Fanshawe.

She edged around the room, circling him. Then, poised near the kitchen door, she suddenly darted from sight. He heard her rummaging out there; drawers clattered. He said in a quiet, patient voice, "Listen to me. Do you remember me from last night? Maybe you think I'm some sort of an official because I came into the jail. I'm Dan Ballard of the Hourglass. Yes, your father tied me up and left me. But it's a mistake. You'll be doing him a favor if you free me. Can't you understand that?"

Again he felt as though he were arguing for his life; the thought, persisting, crept into his voice, putting a strained quality into his pleadings. He thought of threats when his coaxing drew neither word nor action out of her; he decided against that. A girl with the nerve to spring Lew Fanshawe from the Ballardton jail wouldn't be intimidated by a man bound and helpless.

He said at last, angrily, "All right! Leave me here! And if anything happens to me, the Hourglass will pull this place to the ground and hang your father to the highest tree in the Rimfires!"

She appeared in the kitchen doorway. She had a flour sack in her hand; it looked to be loaded with food; he could see the bulking outline of canned foods. She crossed the room quickly, placed the flour sack on the floor near the door and knelt and began fumbling at the knots holding his wrists. Relief turned him weak, but only for a moment. "Get a knife from the kitchen," he said.

She paid him no heed, her fingers still working at the knots. He felt them loosen, and then, suddenly, she ceased her efforts, snatched up the flour sack, opened the door and fled through it. He heard her boots beat against the porch but lost the sound in his wild threshing as he flailed across the floor, struggling to finish the job she'd deserted. He shook his wrists free and tugged quickly at the knots binding his ankles; and all the while he thought, *She's smart — smarter than a whip!* She was on her way to take food to Fanshawe, and she'd guessed that Dan was after the man. This way she was giving Dan his chance and still making sure of her own getaway.

And he had to smile.

All this while he was working frantically; he freed himself and came to a teetering stand; restored circulation sent needles through him, but he was oblivious to the pain. Scooping his gun from the table, he wrenched open the door and thought he caught a glimpse of her plaid shirt in the timber across the clearing. She had come afoot, and she was leaving the same way. He looked for his horse; he had left it tied to the sagging, peeled-pole fence, but the mount was gone. *Of course!* April's surprise at finding him in the house had been proof that his horse was no longer in the yard. He remembered thinking he'd heard the creak of a bit chain after Allison had left; he went running to the barn and found his horse there, standing in a stall, still saddled. He got into the kak and came out of the barn at a high lope, heading for the place in the timber where April had vanished.

The sun hung low, the pine clad sweep of the upper slopes was bathed in gold, and the day's heat had lost its hard impact. He went crashing into the timber, making no effort at stealth, and he found a game trail. He put the horse along it at the same hard run; he kept low in the saddle and held his right arm crooked before his face to ward off the lower branches. He glimpsed her again, around a turn of the trail; she was taking a backward look, her eyes frightened, and she was running. He overtook her, swung down from the saddle and made a grab for her and tripped. Falling, he clutched at one of her ankles and brought her down. Instantly she rolled over, trying to twist free, but he was swarming upon her, pinning her down with his weight. He got his arms around her, trying to pinion hers, and she ceased struggling then, as though the futility of pitting her strength against his had become apparent to her.

Thus there was this moment when she lay in his arms, her black hair fanned out upon the ground, her heart thundering against his, and then, because he wanted to, he kissed her.

There was no intent in this, no forethought; she had just become a woman and desirable, and a wantonness had swept over him and he had surrendered to it. Her lips were warm; he had known only Cynthia, and he hadn't known that a woman's lips could be warm. They were warm and hungry, but that was only for an instant, and then she was fighting him, stark terror in her eyes. She got an arm free and he felt the rake of fingernails along his face. He drew back his head, then got to a stand, pulling her up with him. He locked her wrists behind her and said hoarsely, "You little devil! I'm not going to harm you!"

She was panting hard, her breasts rising and falling. "Let me go!"

"Only if you'll promise not to run," he said, but he released her.

She picked the flour sack from the ground where it had fallen; a can of beans had escaped and she picked this up, too, and restored it to the sack. Dan said, "That's for Fanshawe?"

She made no answer, and he said, "Look, you rode away with him last night. Nobody knows that for sure but me and a friend of mine who'll never tell. I could have put the law on your trail then if I'd wanted to. But I had nothing against you, or against Fanshawe either."

"Then why are you up here today?"

"To try to find him," he admitted. "But not for the reason you think. All I want is to talk to him — ask him a couple of questions. You could take me to him. Will you?"

She said, "He'd kill you!"

He grinned. "He tried that once. That's why he's got a sore shoulder. That bullet could have split his heart if I'd wanted it to. Can't you understand that I mean him no harm? Look at it this way — a great deal of trouble is shaping up on this range. Maybe if I could talk to Fanshawe, there wouldn't be any trouble. Take me to him, April!"

If she was surprised that he knew her name, she didn't show it. She stood a long, long moment in silence; she bit her lower lip and looked at him as though she were trying to inventory the things that didn't show. She owned her father's intelligence, he decided; and he wished now that he hadn't kissed her.

138

He was remembering Cynthia and was ashamed, but he knew, too, that the kiss was counting against him now. It had been no way to build trust.

She said at last, "Give me your gun, and you can come blindfolded. I promise I'll bring you back safe."

Dan almost laughed. What childish game of blindman's buff was this supposed to be? But he said very solemnly, "That sounds fair enough." He lifted his gun and handed it to her; she thrust it into the waistband of her Levis. He unknotted his neckerchief, and she took the bandanna and placed it over his eyes and knotted it at the back of his neck. She said, "Can you see?" At first that struck him as naive, and then, because he understood that she truly trusted him and that her question proved it, he turned humble. He said truthfully, "Only the light when I'm facing toward the sun."

She said, "Just a minute," and he felt her move away. A moment later he could tell that she was leading his horse along the trail toward him. She was busy for a moment — tying the flour sack to the saddle, he supposed — and then she took his hand and placed it upon the saddle horn, and he groped for the stirrup and swung up into the saddle. She said, "Will he carry double?" He said, "I don't know."

She swung up behind him and reached around him for the reins. The horse flinched, and he wondered grimly if he'd have to fight the kinks out of him blindfolded with branches everywhere. He reached to snatch away the bandanna; April drummed her heels against the horse's sides, and the mount started off at a tractable walk.

He was to remember that ride always; it was like moving through a dream. He could hear the squealing of the saddle as the horse toiled up a slant; he could feel a sickening sensation in his stomach when the trail suddenly dipped downward; he could smell the dry tang of the timber, and from these things he tried to visualize the country through which they passed. When they faced west, the sunlight was strong through the bandanna; by this token he was able to tell when they turned north or south. He tried to make a game out of mentally gauging their route, but it was a losing game.

Often April warned him about low-hanging branches, saying softly, "Get your head down." Sometimes he sensed that she reached out and held a branch aside as they passed beneath it. He tried keeping track of time and found that a futile game, too; they might have been riding a half-hour or an hour. Sometimes gravel rattled on the trail, and after a while this sound became persistent, and he wondered if they were out of the timber altogether.

Then April was hauling at the reins, bringing the horse to a stand. She slipped from behind him and said, at his elbow, "Quiet! Riders are near by!" She moved away, and he guessed that she was at the horse's head, her hand clamped over the mount's nostrils to keep him from neighing a greeting.

Dan said quietly, "Who is it?"

"The Cantrells!"

He could hear the passage of horses along a trail; he tried to gauge the distance and the direction and failed at both. He heard the murmur of voices; there was no coherency to this sound, no words he could fasten onto. He smiled, wondering what the Cantrells would think if they should stumble upon the two of them, him sitting a saddle with his hands free but his gun gone and his eyes blindfolded, her standing rigidly, silencing the horse. A sight like that might even sober the old man up! Sound dwindled and was lost. April pulled herself up behind Dan again, and he said, because it was suddenly very important to know, "Were they heading uphill or down?"

"Toward their ranch."

They weren't going to the Hourglass, then. They were waiting out the deadline, waiting to see if the Ballards came to them. It wasn't the showdown — not yet.

The light was fading; he could tell that. Soon only grayness glimmered through the bandanna, and that was brief, the quick twilight of the hill country. Since sundown the gravel had rolled beneath the horse's hoofs, and it seemed to be slower going, as though it were harder to pick the trail. It came to Dan that it had been a long time since April had warned him about a branch; the last time had been before the Cantrells had passed them. He was turning this over in his mind when she brought the horse to a halt again and said, "Get down."

He said, "Now?" and raised his hands to the bandanna.

"Not yet."

He slid to the ground and found rocky underfooting. She said, "Just a minute till I tie your horse to this bush." After that she took his hand and led him along. They climbed upward, and she said, "Careful now. Very careful." He put out his free hand and felt the smoothness of a cliff wall to his right. He pictured himself as climbing a tilting ledge, and something about the picture he conceived tugged at his memory. She said, "Duck your head," and he did so, and for a moment this was like being completely blind; there was only blackness, and then he saw light through the bandanna, a flickering light, and smelled wood smoke. April said, "Now!"

He jerked down the bandanna and found himself in a cave, high and dome-shaped, its ceiling blackened by the smoke of many fires. A fire burned here now, fitful and puny, beneath an opening in the ceiling that made a natural chimney. Before this fire a saddle blanket was spread, and a saddle and other gear lay near by. Other than that the cave was empty, and April, sensing this only now, let the flour sack drop from her hand and cried out in a voice of fear, "Lew! Lew!"

"Here," Lew Fanshawe said behind them, and Dan felt the prod of a six-shooter against his spine.

He raised his hands before turning; he knew now that he stood as close to death as he ever wanted to come; he saw Lew Fanshawe standing in the shoulder-high opening that led into this cave. Fanshawe said, "I heard you coming a mile off. I just moved out and up on the ledge and around a turn, April. I see you've got his gun. Good! What happened? Catch him snooping?"

"I brought him here from the place, Lew," she said. "He only wanted to talk to you."

"You *brought* him here!"

"Blindfolded," she said. "He'll go back the same way."

The anger faded out of Fanshawe's solid features, and a question stood stark in his half veiled eyes. With his free hand he thumbed back his flat-topped sombrero, and then he smiled in feline satisfaction, revealing his teeth. "Back there, Ballard," he said. "Get back and sit down. April, keep away from him."

Dan backed to the blanket and squatted upon it, and Fanshawe followed after him and eased down to the floor a good ten feet away, sitting cross-legged and laying the gun in his lap. Fanshawe said darkly, "Well, you're here. What's eating at you?"

"Two questions," Dan said. "I promised her that's all I'd ask. First, I want to know why you hate me?"

Fanshawe said, "That's easy. Because you're you."

Dan said, "To me that doesn't make sense."

"It wouldn't," Fanshawe said. "It wouldn't because you're not me. You haven't drifted, hiring out your guns and eating well one day and not at all the next. I've sat hungry beside a campfire and thought of men like you — well fed and well kept because somebody else, your father or his father before him, built a pile and all you had to do was be born in order to have it. This isn't the first range where I've seen men bow and scrape before gents like you, just because you were born

144

to a name and a pile of *dinero*. What did you ever do to earn it, Ballard?"

"I see what you mean," Dan said slowly. "And that tells me more than you meant to tell me. Now I know another reason why you hate me. Because I showed myself better than you at your own trade yesterday before the Rialto. I could have killed you, Fanshawe."

Fanshawe's lip curled. "You were lucky," he said. "Plain lucky, Ballard. We'll prove that one of these fine days."

April moved, her shadow dancing a gargantuan dance upon the cave wall. Fanshawe started, his hand dropping to his lap where the gun lay. *He doesn't trust her!* Dan thought. *Not completely.* She picked wood up from a pile and dropped it upon the fire which sprang higher. She moved back to a stand against the wall, saying nothing.

Fanshawe said, "You had a second question, Ballard."

"Yes," Dan said. "Who hired you to keep picking a fight with me?"

Fanshawe smiled. "Sometimes I work for money — sometimes just for fun. In your case it could have been just for fun."

Dan said, "Is that all you'll say?"

"That's it."

Dan started to come to a stand, but Fanshawe's gun was instantly in his hand and lev-

145

eled. Dan said, "I've asked my questions and got my answers. I could have put the law on your trail last night, but I didn't. That was for her sake, not yours. Take my advice and shake the dust of this range."

Fanshawe said, "Stay squatted. You're not going. Not yet."

April said, "He'll be blindfolded when he goes back, Lew. He'll never find this place again — not in a million years."

Fanshawe said, "Look, honey, are you on my side or his?"

It took her a long second to answer. "Yours, Lew," she said softly. "You know that."

She loved the man, Dan reflected. Every time she turned around she proved it.

Fanshawe said, "This is Saturday, isn't it?"

April nodded, and Fanshawe said, "What's your hurry, Ballard? We've food here and a fire — all the comforts of home. No, it's not what you're used to at the Hourglass, but it will do your immortal soul good to come down to the level of us common folks for a while. He's our guest, isn't he, April? For the evening."

Dan saw it then. Fanshawe knew that midnight tonight was the deadline, and he knew that the answer the Cantrells would get from the Hourglass might be one answer if he, Dan, was there and quite another if Wayne was alone. This was part of the game Fanshawe was playing, for himself or somebody else, the game that had started when they'd first met in the Rialto. Dan had played into Fanshawe's hands by coming here, and Fanshawe meant to keep him until after midnight.

And because the Cantrells might be riding at midnight, and because many miles lay between here and the Hourglass and time could work against a man, Dan knew that any play he would make might just as well be made now. He measured the distance between himself and Fanshawe and prepared to leap, yet strong in his consciousness was one thought that couldn't be denied. No man could move faster than a bullet.

11

The Deadline

Some minutes are beyond measuring. This was one of them — this minute when Dan crouched, his legs drawn up under him, his eyes locked with Fanshawe's, and because Fanshawe's intent was suddenly stark in his face, Dan knew that Fanshawe wanted it this way. He wanted Dan to try jumping him, because that would give Fanshawe his excuse to gun Dan down. Fanshawe had a code of sorts to keep, but Dan would free him from it if he made a play! Thinking this, Dan hesitated, his desperate desire tempered by the knowledge that to move was to commit suicide. But anger began wrestling with the wisdom in him, and the mockery in Fanshawe's eyes was a spur to anger.

Then April said, hysteria in her voice, "Drop your gun, Lew!"

Without looking at her, Dan knew how she'd be — her back to the cave's wall, her face contorted by the wrench of emotions, his own gun in her hand, the gun she'd taken from him before she'd brought him here. He still kept his eyes on Fanshawe; he saw surprise take the killer-lust out of Fanshawe, and then fury leaped up in the man, smoldering in his glance, but Fanshawe only said, softly, "And you told me you were on *my* side!"

It was like a whip laid across her. Dan gave her a quick look and saw the way of it, but he saw, too, that the gun she held never wavered. She said, "He made a bargain and he kept it, Lew. He could have pulled the blindfold away any time. When we got here and I told him it was the end of the trail, he could have jumped and come after you, but he didn't. Now I'm going to keep my end of it and take him back."

Fanshawe said, "There's more mixed up in this than you know about. I can't let him leave. Not right away."

The firelight danced upon her face; and she was close to crying. *"Drop that gun, Lew!"* she said with desperate emphasis.

This was the moment when fury rose the highest in Fanshawe. He might have used his gun, or he might have used words, and either could have disarmed her. This was killing April, Dan knew. She loved Fanshawe, but she loved her pledged word, too. The anger that swayed Fanshawe almost engulfed him; his body grew rigid and trembled, and then he let the gun slip from his fingers.

Dan launched himself forward and fell upon the weapon. He plucked Fanshawe's left-hand gun from its holster, and with the two in his hands he broke them open and jacked the cartridges out of them. These he flung to the darkest corner of the cave, and he sent the guns skittering across the floor, and he said, "I ought to take you back with me, but that isn't what she bargained for when she made this play. I told you once to shake the dust of this range. Don't let me lay eyes on you again."

Fanshawe looked at April and said very distinctly, very emphatically, *"You slut!"*

She began crying silently, and the tears shook her voice. "He doesn't know the way to this cave. And I'll take him back blindfolded. Lew, tomorrow you'll be glad I didn't let you do what you intended doing. You just need time to think it over. I'll be back before morning."

He said darkly, "I won't promise I'll be here."

"You can't move till your shoulder's healed better," she said. "And you'll need food and care. Lew, can't you understand that I *have* to do this? Can't you understand that it doesn't need to make a difference between us?"

Dan thought, *No, and he never will!* April believed that goodness lay in Fanshawe because it lay in her. She couldn't understand that there was a difference between them that

150

was wider than Purgatory Gorge.

Dan said, "I'd like to get riding," and started toward the cave's opening.

She followed after him, watching Fanshawe, still holding the gun but letting it hang limply in her hand. Fanshawe had come to a stand; his back was to the fire, and he was blackly outlined and faceless. He said nothing; he made no move. Dan got through the opening, the moon hadn't risen and he was in deep darkness. April crowded close to him and got his hand and said, a sob still in her voice, "This way."

He knew again that he was being led along a tilting ledge, only this time the smoothness of the cliff was to his left. They were descending, and again memory tugged at him, and the picture stood complete, and he smiled. When they came to where the ground was level, the underfooting was still rocky, and he looked upward to the place they had just quit; he saw the blackness of the cliff against the blackness of the night; turning, he made out his horse tied to a bush near by. He untied his bandanna and retied it over his eyes and reached for her hand. "I'm ready now," he said.

He moved toward the horse and groped for the horn and lifted himself aboard; she climbed behind him and put her arms around him and got the reins. For him there was only blackness, deeper than the night's, and that blackness was suddenly peopled by Lew Fanshawe. Fanshawe had had time to find his guns and reload, Dan knew. He had a notion to jerk away the blindfold; it had become a farce anyway, but she didn't know that, and he didn't want her to know it.

They moved for a long time in silence; after an hour she began warning him about trees. He sensed that the moon was rising, and he sensed, too, that they were not traveling the same trail that had brought them to the cave. He listened intently, always, for hoofbeats on the back trail. Fanshawe must have had a horse hidden out near the cave; two of them perhaps. April had come to the hill ranch afoot when she'd come for food that afternoon. He wondered about that, and asked.

"We had two horses," she said. "My own and a Tomahawk horse I took last night. I turned the Tomahawk horse loose in the hills and left the other for Lew when I went for food. He might have needed a horse worse than I did."

That made them even, him and Fanshawe, Dan reflected. With both of them she'd thought of herself last.

Shortly thereafter she said, "Now. You can take away the blindfold." And as she said it she slipped from the horse.

He jerked away the bandanna and had his look. Overhead the blackness of the sky arched, the stars wheeling, and there was moonlight, though most of it was lost in a tangle of pine tops. They were in deep shadow, but just beyond was the openness of a road, bathed a sickly yellow with the ruts grooved in darkness. This was the Tomahawk Pass road; he knew this instantly. April handed him his gun.

He stepped down from the saddle and leaned against the mount, his shoulder to the saddle's cantle. He said, "How long have you known him?"

"Lew?" He thought she was going to cry again. "A month, I guess. Maybe longer. He rode through the hills when he first came into this country. He spent a night near our place, and I stumbled upon him one morning when I was riding. After that, after he went on down to Ballardton, he used to ride up this way once in a while. We found that cave and got to meeting there."

"And so you fell in love with him," he said, "and when you heard he was to be lynched, you found a way to get him out of jail."

"I never thought about the being in love," she said. "Not till last night. I'd heard about your wedding and how everybody was going to be there. I wasn't invited, but I took my horse and rode to town to see the excitement. After he got in trouble and got jailed, I heard the talk. I guess it was too much for me, thinking about him being hanged."

"So you stole a Tomahawk horse for him to ride away on, and you knocked out Abe Potter without Potter's even seeing you. It was Lew Fanshawe's lucky day when he met you."

She lifted her face and looked intently at him and said, "You hate each other, don't you? I wish it weren't that way."

He shrugged. "He'll be clearing out of this range as soon as he's able. Will you be riding away with him?"

"I don't know," she said forlornly. "I don't know whether he'll want me now. Last night he talked about taking me along. But tonight he's angry with me."

He said softly, urgently, "Don't go with him, April."

"You're afraid I'll marry him?"

"No," he said. "I'm afraid he *won't* marry you."

She said nothing; he looked toward the road, conscious that time was slipping away, conscious that the midnight deadline was drawing near. He held out his hand to her; her fingers closed with his, and he drew her close then, very gently, and put his arms around her and tilted her chin and kissed her. She responded willingly; her kiss was a child's kiss in the first moment of it, and then it ceased to be a child's kiss. She pushed away from him, panting. "I guess he's right. I'm just naturally bad!"

At first he thought she meant Fanshawe, and then she said, "Why does he hate me so? Is it just because of her, because of my mother? I've tried not to be like her."

"He's told you about her?"

"Many times. He can lash himself into a fury by talking about her."

He reached out and laid his hand on her shoulder; it was trembling. He said, "You kissed me because you were lonely and mixed-up and afraid that Lew Fanshawe will be gone when you get back to the cave. It will be better for you if he is gone. Will you keep remembering that?"

He stepped up into the saddle again; he prodded the horse out into the road and looked back, seeing April standing at the fringe of the forest, seeing the white blob of her face. He lifted his hand in salute, and a turn of the road put her beyond his view.

After that he tried dismissing her from his mind; tried keeping his faculties pinned to his riding. He needed more light if he were to make speed, but the light was a deceptive thing; the road was day-bright in places and shadow-woven in others where branches swept outward, making an almost tight canopy. He heard the rumble of Purgatory River where the rapids muttered far below; he came to the overhanging rock where he'd looked downward that afternoon and seen Clayton Allison. Remembering the man, he wondered if Allison had returned to the Digby place to find his prisoner gone, and thinking of this, he thought again of April. Poor kid! She had two places to go, two men to go to, and neither really gave a damn about her.

He rode down through the foothills and out upon the flats; now the moon was much higher and the sage clumps stood silvered and the land reached ethereally and endlessly. Hungry, he probed the saddlebag for the remainder of the food and ate while holding the horse to a walk. Afterward he lifted the mount to a gallop; the stars told him midnight was past; he pushed the animal hard, an impatience growing in him. At last he saw the moonlight glinting on the barbed wire that surrounded Ballard Springs. He saw the cattle which crowded close to the wire, and, drawing nearer, he made out the shape of a horse tied to the fence. Not until Dan was close enough to smell the water did he see the man squatting upon the ground, cross-legged. Dan said, "Pete?" tentatively, but it was the voice of Barney Partridge that came back to him.

Partridge said, "I recognized you by the way you sat your saddle." And Partridge took a gun from his lap and eased it back into his holster.

Dan reined short and stepped down from the saddle. "You're spelling Pete? Is this a day and night job?"

"I sent Pete back to the Hourglass," Partridge said.

All the pent-up tension of these many hours put an edge to Dan's voice. "Damn it, man, is something up?"

"Not yet," Partridge said. "When I came in from riding fence today, the ranch was as peaceful as a Ladies' Aid meeting. But Wayne had been working with pen and paper. I took a look at that paper. It was lying on the table."

Dan thought, *I can guess!*

He said, "An agreement to turn Ballard Springs over to the Cantrells?"

Partridge nodded. "Maybe he was just drawing it up in case. Maybe he didn't intend to use it unless he had to. Maybe he was waiting for you to show back."

"I got delayed," Dan said dryly. "The Cantrells haven't come?"

"Not yet," Partridge said. "They'll be coming anytime now. But they'll have to come this way."

Understanding smote Dan then, hitting him hard. "And that's why you're waiting here?" he ejaculated.

Partridge said, "I'm only the foreman. It ain't for me to say whether papers are to be signed or not. But nobody gave me any real orders. If a ruckus was to start between *me* and the Cantrells *before* they reached the Hourglass, it might blow the lid off without any palaver about papers. Maybe I overstepped myself. Do I draw my time, Dan?"

What was it Gramp had said about this man? "Then Barney Partridge could have given you a better lesson than any you got from your Eastern teachers. He's out in the bunkhouse these days, eating his heart out because the spread he's worked for would rather sidestep than fight Cantrell —"

Dan looked at Partridge, seeing a little man, short and stocky, and warped by too much riding, seeing a man loyal to his brand and loyal to something else, to a principle that allowed for no running when a challenge was laid down.

"Draw your time?" Dan said. "Not if I've got any say, you won't. Pile on your horse, Barney. We're heading for the Hourglass. We'll do our talking to the Cantrells there —

when they show up. If there's a fight, you'll get your share of it. But a Ballard is going to have the privilege of starting it."

Partridge grinned. "You saddle it; I'll ride it," he said.

Dan stiffened. "Hoofbeats!" he said. "Hear them?"

Partridge listened. "From the south," he decided. "It's not the Cantrells. Just one rider."

"I see him now," Dan said.

The hoofbeats grew louder; the horse and rider shaped up like a charging fury, the man, tall and angular, sitting unsteadily in the saddle, weaving to and fro in such a way that Dan's first thought was that Clayton Allison was wounded. Then, as the man blurred past them, so intent upon his riding that he didn't even glance in their direction, some instinct told Dan the real truth. Allison was drunk, so drunk he could scarcely sit his saddle.

Partridge said, "He'll break his fool neck once he gets into the hills."

Dan said softly, "So he needed whisky to nerve himself for the job. Is that what took him away from Digby's?" Then, to Partridge, "Let's be riding, Barney. We've got worries of our own."

12

Came the Cantrells

The moon was gone and the stars nearly faded when they came to the Hourglass; the ranch lay cradled in the darkness before the dawn; the buildings were vague and shapeless, but the dogs were awake, and there was a light in the bunkhouse and another in the frame ranch house. Sleep hadn't come here; Dan could feel the wakefulness that pervaded the place; it sang in the night, it was a wire drawn tight and thrumming. A man shaped up in the bunkhouse door as they dismounted, the bulk of him almost blotting out the light. He held a rifle in the crook of his arm, and he had his look and sighed explosively, and said, "Oh, it's you, Barney!"

Dan said, "Will you take care of my horse, Barney? It looks like Wayne is still up."

Wayne was in the big room, burrowed deep in a chair before the empty fireplace. He had hauled off his boots, but otherwise he was clothed; he looked haggard; he looked like a man who could use a drink but would find one drink not enough. Standing in the doorway and studying his brother, Dan reflected that Wayne had never been more than a sociable drinker, a fellow who hoisted one with the crew and walked away afterward and forgot about it. He was glad now that it was this way with Wayne. He said, "Good morning."

Wayne started visibly, and said with an edge of irritation to his voice, "Where the hell have you been? I've been thinking of sending the crew looking for you!"

Dan thought, *But you were afraid to do that. You were afraid to have the ranch unmanned.* He said, "My yarn will keep. Anything happened here?"

"Ransome Price rode out. He offered to buy the place for some investors who are interested. They want to make it a vacation spot for Easterners. His offer was a good one, considering the drought."

Dan crossed to the table. A pen lay there, and an ink bottle, and a piece of paper. He read what Wayne had written upon this paper, and he said, "Price's offer wasn't so good that you'd prefer to take it and run out. All this needs to give Cantrell what he wants is three signatures."

Wayne said, "How did I know whether you'd get back before the Cantrells came? I expected them at midnight. I had to have that ready in case it was needed."

Dan said, "You couldn't have gotten a majority. You'd never have got Gramp to sign it."

Wayne's jaw grew tight. "I'd have signed it myself, if I had to. I can't see where Gramp's vote counts for much any more. And you weren't here."

Dan grinned. "You tell Gramp that."

Wayne made an angry gesture with his hands. "We've got two choices. We can sell to Price, or we can stay here and buck Cantrell. That's all there is to it."

"We've got a third choice," Dan said. "We can fight. That will be Gramp's vote, and it will be mine." He tore the sheet of paper across, folded it and tore it again, and let the pieces flutter to the table. He turned and started for the stairs, and Wayne said desperately, "Where are you going?"

"To bed," Dan said. "The Cantrells hoped we'd come riding to them. They wanted that feather for their hat, too. Midnight is past, and they haven't come. They won't come until tomorrow. I need sleep."

That one step creaked under him as he climbed the stairs. Gramp's door was closed and no light showed under it. In his own room, Dan stripped off his boots and belt and stretched himself upon the bed. All the weariness of the crowded days since his homecoming rose and engulfed him. He thought

162

of April and wondered if she was back at the cave and how she was faring with Fanshawe. The thought was bitter and the thought was sweet, and he took it with him into sleep, into oblivion.

He awoke many hours later to the touch of Wayne's hand. Wayne was shaking him and the heat lay heavy in the room and the sun beat at the window. He looked up at Wayne and wished that Wayne would go away, and then, as clarity penetrated into his sleep-fogged mind, he said, "The Cantrells?"

Wayne said, "Cynthia's coming. I spotted her to the south through field glasses. No, the Cantrells haven't showed up yet. I let you sleep. You were sleeping like a dead man."

Dan said, "Thanks. I'll be down pronto."

She had just reached the gate when he got to the gallery, his face raw from hasty shaving, his hair slicked down and still wet. She rode a livery-stable horse with a stock saddle, but she sat it side-saddle fashion, her skirts billowing. He came running and reached and got her under the armpits and eased her to the ground. She was once again coolness in a parched land, minted gold to an impoverished lover; but the memory of their talk at her father's gate, the bargain they'd struck, put a restraint into him. He laughed to cover the awkwardness that had crept into this moment,

163

and he said, "I slept in. Will you have a second breakfast with me?"

She was graver than he'd ever remembered her. She said, "I had to come out to learn how things are. The whole town is wondering this morning. You see, everyone knew last night was the deadline."

"The Cantrells haven't come for their answer," he said. "They'll be along before the day's over, I'm guessing. Come to the gallery where there's a little shade. Will you have that second breakfast?"

"Perhaps a cup of tea," she said. "No one on Purgatory Range can make tea like Charley Wong."

Wayne greeted her as Dan led her up the steps. Wayne gave her his hand and said, "You'll find the house a little cooler than the yard, but not much. Lord, will this heat ever let up?"

Dan went seeking Charley Wong; afterward Dan and Cynthia and Wayne sat in the big room, and this made it a state occasion. For Wayne it was the midday meal, but Wayne had no relish for the food; his lack of appetite was all too noticeable. Only Charley, who served, was himself; Cynthia had always charmed him, and her magic had lost none of its potency. She drank the tea and said then, "You can understand why all the folks are waiting to find out what decision is reached about the springs. It means so much to everyone."

Including Ransome Price, it seems, Dan thought.

He said, "How would you vote, Cyn, if it were up to you?" He hadn't meant to ask that; it was a reaching out to older days, an attempt to recapture a closeness that had once existed among the three of them. Often they'd sat in this very room and talked about Dan's proposed schooling and spun plans and dreams, and Cynthia had been as much a part of the Hourglass as those hewn rafters overhead. Dan thought, *I wonder if it will ever be that way again,* and wondering, he awaited her answer.

She pursed her lips thoughtfully and took a long time at replying, and she said then, "I just don't know. But bloodshed seems so useless."

He had known somehow that her answer would be like this, yet he'd hoped it would be different. He could hear a clock ticking; he made a guess at the time and wondered when the Cantrells would be coming and found himself wishing that she'd leave before they arrived. But she lingered; the three of them made small talk, and time drifted on, and the heat built with the passing hours. It grew to envelop the house, to press it with hot hands; a stickiness dwelt in the air, and Wayne, who'd worn his coat to the table as a concession to Cynthia's presence, stripped the garment away. A thermometer was fastened out on the gallery; Wayne went to have a look at it and returned shaking his head, making no pronouncement. And then Barney Partridge clumped up the gallery's steps and stood in the doorway looking at the three of them, a little man freighted with news.

"Riders to the north. Six of 'em. They've come."

Dan said, "Cyn, you'd better stay inside!"

But she followed him to the gallery, and Wayne came along, too. Wayne took a stand at Dan's left shoulder, Partridge ranged himself to the right; the three of them were this way, standing, waiting out the last tag-end of waiting, when the Cantrells roared into the yard. The six lined up before the gallery, sitting their saddles, the old man and his sons, and Wayne said nothing and Dan said nothing; there was no invitation for the Cantrells to light down. But Dan thought, *So this is it.*

Old Man Cantrell sat with his sons on either side of him. He had more than enough whisky in him today, and more than enough petulance. He sat there, big and burly, with his ragged beard falling to his second shirt button;

166

he sat there arrogant and dangerous; and he said, "Midnight is a helluva long ways past, Ballard. Did you think we were bluffing?"

He was speaking to Wayne, and Wayne made the answer. "We've thought it over. The Tomahawk is welcome to water cows at the springs, the same as anybody else. But we're not signing over the springs to you."

"You've thought that over damn' well?"

"We've thought it over," Wayne said stiffly. "You've got our answer."

Cantrell said, "I tried to make it easy for you, Ballard. Hourglass and Tomahawk could have got through this dry spell together. But you wouldn't listen to sense. We're heading back to the hills. To get our crew and round up our cattle to fetch 'em down to the flats. We're taking over Ballard Springs."

The anger that ran away with Dan was compounded of both ice and fire; he had known another moment like this, that moment when Lew Fanshawe had spat upon his boot in Ballardton the day of the postponed wedding. He said in a voice that sounded strange in his ears, "That's enough, Cantrell!"

Cantrell said, "Another county heard from!"

"You got decent treatment from the Hourglass, Cantrell," Dan said. "That wasn't enough for you. You've wanted to hog the water. You had the guts to set a deadline for the Ballards, to expect us to ride up to the Tomahawk and grovel because you happened to growl. You've got the guts now to sit there and tell us you're taking over our water. I'm here to tell you you're not that wide across the britches. You can still water your quota of cattle — no more, no less. I wouldn't want to see a cow suffer because the man who owns him is stupider than the cow. Now get off Hourglass land and stay off!"

Cantrell's five sons had held silent; this was their way, to let their father do the talking. Now Mace spoke. He was the one who sat at his father's right hand; he was neither the oldest nor the youngest of the sons; he was thirty, perhaps, but he was the biggest of the five. He was Old Man Cantrell with a quarter of a century sloughed away. His was his father's arrogance and his father's ruthlessness. He said, "He talks big for an Eastern dude, Paw. He's the one who talked Wayne into bucking us. He's grown a set of guts because he was lucky with a gun in town the other day. Shall I haul him over to his own horse trough and cool him off, Paw?"

Dan said, "Will you climb down off that horse, Mace? Will you climb down and shuck your gun?"

From farther along the gallery where Cynthia had taken a stand, her voice rose. She said, *"Don't!"* but it was a puny straw to stem the tide of Dan's anger. He cleared the gallery steps without touching them. He crossed to where Mace Cantrell sat his saddle, and he got his hand inside Mace's gun belt and hauled the man from the saddle, and he slapped Mace hard, his fingers leaving red streaks across the man's face.

Mace fell back a pace, looking at Dan with eyes that didn't believe, looking at him with anger that grew and boiled over and exploded. He fumbled woodenly at his gun belt and un-latched it and let it fall. He came at Dan with a roar, his huge fists flailing, a berserk animal filled with one consuming lust. Dan caught him full in the mouth with his left fist; he buried his right in Mace's body just above the belt line. He heard the gusty wheeze that came out of Mace; he saw the man's head snap back.

He bored at Mace again, but this was Dan's mistake. There was too much resiliency in that mass of bone and muscle; anger might have made Mace clumsy, but it hadn't lessened his power. His fist caught Dan above the ear, fill-ing his head with a wild buzzing; Dan went down to his knees and, falling, clung grimly to consciousness. He saw Mace bearing down upon him, a wild triumph in the man's face.

Dan lowered his head as a bull does; he caught Mace in the midriff and broke that charge, and this gave Dan time to get to his feet again.

Now it became a wild trading of blows; some instinct whispered to Dan that he must keep Mace at a distance; he mustn't let Mace wrap those great arms around him or get him to the ground where weight could make all the difference. He was content then merely to fend off Mace; he did this by raining blows upon Mace, but he took blows in return, and there was a rock-like quality to Mace's fists. For Dan, the world had narrowed to this man; he was only remotely aware that the other Cantrells had pulled back their horses, giving them ground before the gallery in which to fight. He knew the Cantrells were cheering on their kinsman; he could hear the voices, but could make no coherence out of the words. His own supporters were on the gallery; he had a blurred impression of Wayne's face and Partridge's, and he saw Cynthia, a white mask of a face. Why hadn't she stayed inside like he'd told her to do?

That stolen look almost cost him the fight; he had this one unguarded moment and Mace's fist caught him high and hard again, and his legs tangled, and he went down. He saw Mace come at him; he saw Mace's boot rise to kick him in the ribs; he clutched desperately at that boot and twisted, hoping to bring Mace to the ground. Mace fell and Dan rolled over on top of him and they were a writhing mass, and Dan felt the man's finger at his throat and the man's thumb trying for his eyes.

Out of the dust and the chaos he heard a strident, lifting cry. *"Get to your feet, you damn fool. You've got no chance on the ground!"*

He thought, *That's Gramp!* and wondered how Gramp had got to the gallery. He'd fought this fight to keep himself out of Mace's grip, but desperation and tiredness and pain had robbed him of wisdom. Now he knew again what he had to do, because Gramp had just told him. He got Mace beneath him and broke free of Mace and struggled to a stand. He was reeling unsteadily on his feet, his fists cocked, when Mace clumsily arose. He let Mace get up, but gave Mace no more time than that; he came at Mace with the last shreds of his power concentrated on the task and the need. He flung his fist at Mace's jaw; he felt his knuckles smash against that jaw; he saw Mace go down and lie in the dust of the yard with his arms outflung and his legs twisted, making no move.

Dan stepped back, sobbing for breath; his shirt was a ruin and one eye was swollen and his lips hurt. He stepped back, calling hoarsely to Mace to arise and not understanding why Mace didn't. He turned and looked toward the gallery; Barney Partridge had a gun out and level in his hand; Hourglass's foreman was as he'd been that day in the Rialto when he'd broken up Lew Fanshawe's play. Partridge said, "All right, Cantrell. Pick up your man and hang him across his saddle. Dan's already told you everything you need telling. Now git!"

Old Man Cantrell looked toward where Mace lay; he looked and was a man who saw but could not comprehend what he saw. He climbed heavily from the saddle and crossed to Mace and dragged at one of Mace's arms. "Git up, you damn' fool," he said with disgust. Then, to his other sons, "Hob — Ring — give me a hand."

Dan didn't watch them load Mace upon the horse. He was only vaguely conscious of their spurring their mounts and galloping out of the yard. He was looking toward the gallery; he saw Barney Partridge, a man grown in stature in these last few minutes; he saw Wayne, and in Wayne's eyes was sympathy for a brother hurt, sympathy and a new respect. He saw Cynthia, but he didn't want to look at Cynthia; he didn't like the sick horror in her face; he didn't like remembering that he had put it there. He saw Gramp leaning upon his cane.

172

Partridge said, "That's that. But they'll be back, just like they said, with all their cows trailing along. Just a minute, Dan; I'll help you up the steps. What came over you? If ever I saw a man licked it was you when Mace got you down. Yet you broke away from him and laid him out. I'd like to know about that."

"Ask Gramp," Dan said.

He looked at Gramp and saw Gramp's grin, and he grinned in return, a broken, battered grin. He took a step forward and the ground seemed to tilt and the horizon to revolve. It was too damn' hot today, he decided. He would have fallen except that both Partridge and Wayne were suddenly there beside him, giving him something to lean against.

13

A Ride to Make

They got Dan up to the gallery and inside the house; they eased him into one of the chairs in the big room. It was good to sit down; it was good to let the chair hold him; it soothed the pain that spread through him. He looked at his knuckles; they were skinned and bloody, and he wondered if they were broken.

Wayne said, "Where the devil is Charley? We'll need hot water."

Barney Partridge said, "And a piece of beefsteak for that eye."

Gramp came limping in; he stood to one side of the doorway, leaning heavily on his cane. Out of his chair and with the blanket gone from around his legs, he looked a great deal thinner to Dan, but his face wasn't as gray as Dan had remembered it. There was a fire in Gramp. There was a new vigor to him. He frowned at Dan and said, "Didn't you know better than to try tangling with a bigger man on the ground? You were lucky today — just plain lucky."

Dan said, "I licked him, Gramp; you know doggone well I did."

"Bah!" said Gramp. "You don't know any

more about handling your fists than a steer knows about square dancing!"

"To hell with you, Gramp," Dan said softly and grinned, but it hurt his lips to grin.

Cynthia came in and stood near the doorway. In this past moment Dan had forgotten about Cynthia. She came as a ghost comes, soundless and pale. She said in a small voice, "I'll have to be going back to town."

Dan said, "Give me a few minutes to take the kinks out of myself and I'll ride with you."

She looked at him in stark horror; she had looked at him in this manner once before — that moment when she'd lain in her father's office in her wedding gown and had opened her eyes to see him standing over her with Barney Partridge's gun hot in his hand. She was afraid of him! She was as much afraid of him as though he were Lew Fanshawe or Mace Cantrell, or someone like that! Thinking this, he was sure he had lost her forever, and the regret drove deep into him and was more painful than the havoc Mace's fist had wrought.

He said, "I'm sorry you had to see the fight, Cyn."

The revulsion was still in her eyes, but anger came there, too. She said, "It was so brutal, and so unnecessary. You'd made your say, and the Cantrells understood you. Just because that big hulk made a childish challenge, you didn't have to be like a schoolboy who'd had a chip knocked from his shoulder."

He said forlornly, "You don't understand, Cyn. You just don't understand."

"And I'm afraid I never will. Not long ago I said that you seemed to attract violence. Now I know that you go out looking for it."

Wayne had gone elsewhere in the house. Dan had heard his voice calling out for Charley; he had heard this without hearing it. Wayne shaped up in the doorway; he looked at Cynthia and said, an edge of annoyance to his voice, "He's just had the stuffings pounded out of him. I think that any talk about it can keep till later."

Charley came in, his face ludicrous with concern. He bore a piece of beefsteak, and his yellowed hands forced Dan back in the chair, and he laid the beefsteak upon Dan's left eye. He had a cloth with him, wrung out in cold water, and he placed this upon Dan's face, molding it carefully around his nose.

Wayne said, "We'll want to get those hands of yours into water and stop the knuckles from swelling." Dan felt Wayne's fingers on his knuckles and winced. "Nothing broken, I guess," Wayne said.

Dan could sense that all of them were hovering about him. He heard a flurry of hoofbeats out in the yard and half-raised himself from the chair. Wayne said, "That's Cynthia. She's gone toward town. Take it easy, kid. You can square yourself with her later."

Dan said, "I did it up brown all around." The cloth was lifted from his face, iodine stung at the open cuts, and the cloth was replaced. His knuckles were being wrapped. Dan said, "Well, we gave Cantrell his answer, and we blew the lid right off. You did the speaking, Wayne, but I'm the gent who made up your mind for you."

Wayne said, "It doesn't matter."

"You're not sorry?"

"It's like a load was lifted from my shoulders, Dan. I guess the tough part of it was not knowing what to do — that and waiting for the deadline to draw nearer. Now that the choice has been made, I feel like a free man. It's a good feeling. We know what we're up against."

Dan said, "You're a good man, Wayne."

Wayne said gruffly, "We'll get you over to the couch where you can stretch out. No, leave that cloth on your face. We'll help you."

The move was made, and Dan eased himself upon the couch and someone tugged at his boots and removed them. He heard that one step creak, and he said, "Gramp?"

"Gone back upstairs, Dan. I guess he can't

stand being on his feet too long at a stretch."

Dan said, "You can't fool around here, messing with me. We've got to get ready for a fight. Cantrell will bring his cattle down from the hills, just as he said he would."

Partridge's voice came from somewhere near by. Hourglass's foreman said, "We can beat the Tomahawk to the gun. We can carry the war into the hills."

"No," Dan said. "He'll have to start it, if he wants his fight. Barney, you'd better move the whole crew to Ballard Springs. Have Charley fetch the chuck wagon out there. We'll guard the water and wait it out. If Cantrell brings his cattle, he'll find us ready to fight."

Partridge said, "I'm on my way. How many rifles we got around this place?"

Wayne said, "Charley can take care of you, Dan. I'll go see what I can do to help Barney."

He heard Wayne's boots beat toward the doorway; the room turned silent, and a fly buzzed somewhere. This was the hottest part of the day; the heat smothered Dan, surrounding him and gluing his clothes to him. He grew drowsy; he fought against sleeping; there was so much that needed to be done. He could hear an anarchy of sound out in the yard; horses squealing and men calling to one another. His spread was riding to war, while he was lying here like a newborn baby! He resolved to be on his feet and ready to go with them before they stepped up into saddles. He was conscious of Charley's coming with fresh cloths for his face and knuckles. And then, in spite of himself, he slept.

He awoke and there was darkness, and he spent a moment wondering what time it was. The darkness came from the cloth over his eyes; he reached and took it away and remembered April and those two blindfolded rides through the hills. He sat up and found the gray of twilight in the room. The house still held some of the day's heat, and he arose and walked to the gallery, and the coolness there was like a benediction. His body was not as sore as he'd supposed it would be. He wondered how Mace Cantrell felt, and knew a certain sympathy, not having any hate in him. He came back into the big room and discovered bread and cold meat upon the center table. Good old Charley! He tugged on his boots and ate the food and felt better.

The ranch lay swathed in silence; he went out into the yard and found bunkhouse and cook-shack empty, and the chuck wagon gone from the shed. He got a rope and went to the corral and laid a noose over the neck of a horse and got gear onto the mount. It was labor to get this done, and pain climbed with him into the saddle. He headed north, holding the horse to an easy gait. He looked back and saw no light showing in the ranch house, not even in Gramp's room.

He had much to think about on that ride toward the springs, but his thoughts centered on April and from them grew a need for a decision. This he tried putting from his mind. He remembered her as last he'd seen her, standing beside the pass road there on the fringe of the forest; he remembered Lew Fanshawe and Clayton Allison. But what kind of damn' fool notions were these? He'd started a war for his outfit today, and they were ahead, at the springs, waiting for the Tomahawk to strike. There was nothing he could do for April; she'd doomed herself the day she'd set eyes on Lew Fanshawe. She'd ride away with Fanshawe because that's the way it was with her. He, Dan, couldn't live her life for her.

He put his horse to a gallop, trying to outrun his thoughts. He came across the flatness with the dusk closing in on him and the hills losing their shape and the first stars showing. Soon he saw the firelight ahead; he'd expected that the crew might have a fire going, but there were three fires, spaced a few dozen yards apart. As he drew nearer he made out the high outline of the chuck wagon, and then saw there were two other wagons as well, and a good many more men lined against the fires than drew Hourglass pay. He didn't understand this at first; but when he rode into the group he recognized faces and responded to greetings. Four outfits were represented here — the Hourglass, the Circle-Bar, the Hashknife and the Wagon Wheel.

Dan stepped down from his saddle in a knot of men and said, "Where's Wayne?"

Wayne said, "Here, kid," and came shouldering toward him.

Dan grinned bleakly and said, "The news got around, didn't it?"

Wayne said, "Cynthia must have made a fast ride to town and the word went winging from there. That kind of news was bound to travel fast. Jim Satterwaite met her on the road south. Him and his Wagon Wheel outfit were here before we showed up. The rest came later."

Dan said, "Send them back to their spreads, Wayne."

Wayne shook his head. "I don't grab onto that, Dan. They're here to help us."

"Send them back," Dan insisted. "It's our fight."

"But they've got a stake here, too, kid. It means no water for them if Cantrell grabs the springs. Dan, I just don't understand you! A couple of nights back you were burning leather into town to save Fanshawe from being

lynched. You talked about a spark and a powder keg then; you said that the lynching might
blow the lid off. Then you held out to fight
Cantrell, and that really lifted the lid. Now
you want to turn fighting men away."

Dan said, "It's our water, and it's our fight.
Yes, I know we'll be fighting so that the rest
of them can use the water. But the thing I've
been afraid of ever since I got home is a full-
sized range war. Today it shaped up as a fight
between two spreads — the Hourglass and
the Tomahawk. Let these men stay, and Cantrell will have more than he can chew. The
next thing, he'll be importing gunmen by the
trainload. He'll be doing that because we'll
be giving him no choice when we stack the
odds against him. Then we'll have red hell
loose on this range. Send these men back,
Wayne."

Barney Partridge made an unobtrusive appearance at Dan's elbow. Partridge said, "He's
right, Wayne."

Gramp Ballard said, "Of course he's right!
I tried to tell you the same thing, Wayne, when
we first rode up and found the Wagon Wheel
here. But you didn't even savvy what I was
driving at."

Dan said, *"Gramp!"* in vast astonishment.
"What the devil are *you* doing here?"

Wayne spread his hands in a weary gesture.

182

"It was his own idea. I tried to talk him out of it. He ordered Barney to saddle up a horse for him, and Barney did. I thought Gramp would fall off it before we got here."

Dan said sternly, "You can pile on that horse again, Gramp, and go home."

Gramp said, "This is Ballard Springs, and I'm a Ballard. What you said about the others doesn't hold for me."

Dan said, "There's one thing you might as well get straight right now, Gramp. I give the orders here. Or Wayne gives them. And you've got your orders. Get back to the ranch where you belong."

They looked at each other across the space that lay between them, and they were never more alike than in this moment. It was not only a likeness of tallness and looseness and height of forehead; they were alike in their stubborn determination, and they were pitted now, one against the other, and it had never happened before, not like this. Dan expected anger; he saw it building in Gramp's eyes. He expected abuse; he saw it trembling on Gramp's lips. There was this one long-drawn-out moment when yesterday glared across a distance at today; when age stood ready to dispute the way with youth.

Then Gramp said, "I got to rest a while before I can make that ride back. Confound it, Dan, you know I ain't as young as I used to be. You ought to show some respect for my years."

Dan said, "You're laughing inside you, damn you." He crossed and laid a gentle hand on Gramp's shoulder. "You know you can't handle a rifle and a cane at the same time. And somebody had better be at the ranch, Gramp. You know that."

Gramp said angrily, "Tell me right out that I'm too old for fighting. Boss me around just because I ain't got the strength to turn you over my knee. I'm a helluva long ways from dead yet!"

Dan said, "You can hit me with the cane again, Gramp, if it'll make you feel better."

A grin grew on Gramp's face. "I don't need to. It already turned the trick. I wish your dad was here to see you tonight, Dan."

Wayne said, "Somebody riding up. From the south."

Gramp looked and said, "It's a mite early for the vultures to be gathering."

Ransome Price rode into the rim of firelight; he sat his horse well, and his back was straight, but the dust of hard traveling was upon him. He gave no greeting; he said, "I got the news from Cynthia, so I came out. It's to be war, is that it?"

Dan walked toward Price; anger stirred in

Dan, and he said, "Cynthia rode fast, and you rode fast. I'm wondering just how long it's been since you started patterning yourselves after each other."

Price frowned; the firelight washed across his face and made a mask of it. "The news became common property. I'm here on business, Ballard, not to discuss personalities. I made Wayne an offer yesterday. He had to talk it over with you. There's still a way out of this fight. Sell the Hourglass to the people I represent and it won't matter about Ballard Springs. You can stop the bloodshed."

Dan said softly, "Now I know who's been doing Cynthia's thinking for her!"

Gramp said, "I gave him his answer, Dan. Yesterday."

A revulsion grew in Dan, and he wanted Price out of his sight. Dan said, "What Gramp told you should have been enough, Price. You're wasting your time. And ours."

For a moment the mask was stripped away and the studied affability was gone out of Price, and he said harshly, "I've waited a long time to see the highhandedness taken out of you Ballards. I won't have to wait much longer. When the Cantrells have beaten you to your knees, come crawling to me and I'll trade you railroad tickets for what's left of the Hourglass."

"You'd better go," Dan said coldly.

Silence hung over the crowded men of four ranches, and from this silence an animosity arose that was almost a clamor. It beat against Price, not moving him, not for a long moment. Then Price wheeled his horse about; he used his spurs savagely and the silence broke to the beat of hoofs, and the night claimed him.

A man cursed and said, "Well, he shore showed which side of the fence he's on."

Dan thought, *And now the cards are faced — all of them.* A weight had been lifted from him, and he knew now how Wayne had felt today when the Cantrells had come and the piece had been spoken and the die had been cast.

He walked to his own horse and hauled himself into the saddle and looked down at Wayne, who had followed him. "I've got a ride to make," Dan said. "There's something that needs doing. The way I figure it, the Cantrells won't come before late tomorrow; they'll need that much time to comb their cattle out of the hills. I'll be back before then."

Wayne said, "You're not heading north again?"

Dan nodded. "I suppose I should tell you why I'm going, especially at a time like this. There aren't any words which would make it sound like sense — not even to me. When

I come back, I'll try telling you about it. Meanwhile, see that Gramp gets home, will you, Wayne? He'll try to outfox you. He wants to be in on the fight."

Wayne said, "I can't let you ride away like this, kid. If there's a reason why you mustn't take me along, take Barney."

Dan said, "It's my affair, and I've got to ride alone. Do you remember Sam Digby's place very well, Wayne? Remember that cave back in the hills, a few miles west of his house? I found it when I was first old enough to go riding alone, and I used to call it the Pirate's Cave and go there to play. Mind the time when it rained so hard and I had to stay there all night, and you and Barney came looking for me the next morning?"

"I remember," Wayne said.

"I'm going to that cave, Wayne. If something happens and I'm not back by tomorrow, you can send Barney there after me."

Fear built in Wayne's eyes, but it was not for himself. That was the difference today had made in Wayne. He said, "You'll be riding almost to the Tomahawk fence. You'll be shot out of the saddle if the Cantrells sight you. Dan, do you have to make this ride?"

"That's the hell of it," Dan said. "I *do* have to make it. And I couldn't tell you why, because I don't know myself."

14

Allison

Clayton Allison, riding northward past Ballard Springs the night before, had not seen Barney Partridge and Dan Ballard by the barbed wire, for Allison, as Dan had surmised, was a man too drunk to be in command of his faculties. He had had a tiring, nerve-wracking day, had Allison. He had descended to the bottom of Purgatory Gorge, a feat to take the stomach out of a man, and engaged in certain observations down there; and he had made the ascent to return to the Digby place to find Dan Ballard prowling about. He had got Dan under a gun and tied Dan, and that was when the worry had really begun — the worry and the need for a decision.

His life had been a life of making decisions. But they had been impersonal decisions; they involved mountains and rivers, and there was a good education in engineering to help him make these decisions. With people it was different. He had never known people, not really. He had been shy and scholarly as a boy; he was the autumn child of parents who had no other children. He had married a woman who was his opposite in every respect; he had loved her with the ardor of the love-starved and had the heart burned out of him when she'd run away with another man. No person had owned any part of Allison's affection after that; he had grown bitter and cynical and more brooding with each year. He had grown away from people and more uncertain of himself, and today he'd looked at Dan Ballard, trussed and helpless upon the floor, and seen in Ballard the shape of calamity and known what had to be done. He had known, and turned his face from the hideous truth, the hideous need. He had wanted another to make the decision.

And so he had ridden hard to Ballardton and come to the office of Ransome Price.

They had talked for a long time, he and Price, though mostly Price had talked and he had listened. Price had spoken of many things, a prize at stake, the need for a man to be strong when the stake was so high, the inevitability in what had to be done. Price had argued and Price had threatened, and Price had pointed out that when a man got a certain length along a certain trail there was no turning back. Price had been logical, and an engineer could understand logic and make no defense against it. In the end, Price had said what he'd said at the beginning. "Ballard's got to die. There isn't any choice about it. I'm as sorry as you are, Allison, but we can't risk his knowing. And all the signs say that he knows."

Whereupon Clayton Allison had set himself to the task of getting very drunk before riding back to the hills.

He had never been a drinking man. He had lived in rough camps on the far fringes of the frontier. His work had taken him to such places, and he had known all the cravings of men who live too much alone. But he had been master of himself. He could take the passed bottle, or he could leave it alone. He had been toasted by soft-handed, well-dressed men who put up the money for the engineering projects that were given birth by his skill. He had drunk the toast and tossed his glass over his shoulder and thought no more about it. But tonight had been different.

He had stood at one bar and another, drinking morosely, talking to no one. He had drunk, and his tiredness and his bitterness had been his allies at the task. He had ridden out of Ballardton scarcely able to sit in his saddle, and he toted a quart of Valley Tan in his saddlebag, knowing he would need this reserve to sustain himself across the miles to the work that had to be done.

The riding had sobered him a little, and he'd almost got sick. When he felt sobriety coming upon him, he uncorked the bottle he carried. He made a game out of doling it out; he'd ridden to Ballardton too many times not to know all the landmarks, and he had a drink at the prairie-dog village and promised himself another when he was beyond the Hourglass. He took his third drink as he began climbing into the hills; they were deep, hearty pulls, those drinks; they burned down into him, and the fumes rose and numbed his brain again, and that was good. He thought, *Why, this is how a man really gets away from the world! He climbs inside his own skull and peers out through his eyes!*

He almost met with disaster upon the trail up Tomahawk Pass. He was pushing the horse hard, and he took a sharp turn in this fashion and might have sent the mount headlong into the timber; but the animal balked, and Allison's chin snapped hard against his chest. He shook his head and was cold sober for a moment; he took another pull at the bottle and let the horse choose its own gait. He thought, "Got to be careful," and was surprised to find that he'd muttered it aloud.

After that, he dozed in the saddle, and he might have missed the turnoff to Digby's, but the horse, out of long habit, took to the road Digby had cleared, and Allison awoke to find himself in the stump-mottled space before the log house that was now his home. The house lay dark; and that was as he'd expected. He had not seen his daughter for two days, and he was suddenly cold with a certainty that he would never see her again. Yet he was glad she had not come home; he was glad and sorry and all mixed up, and he turned to the bottle again. He drank steadily, holding the bottle up to the moonlight and gauging the fall of its contents. He climbed down from the horse, letting the mount stand, and went groping into the barn, almost stumbling.

He thought, *I'm too drunk to hit the floor with my hat!* He had heard a man say that somewhere once, and it had sounded very inane; now it seemed hilariously funny, and he wanted to laugh, but he couldn't. He giggled, and his hands went probing in a certain corner, and he found a shovel and a lantern.

Some instinct told him to light the lantern outside. He'd have to be careful or he'd burn down the barn. He came to the doorway and got the lantern burning, and thus he never noticed that Dan Ballard's horse was gone. This would have made all the difference to him; this would have told him that Ballard no longer lay tied in the house. He went walking, with the lantern swinging in one hand, the whisky bottle in the other, and the shovel tucked under his arm. His shadow scissored beside him; it was a silly-looking shadow and he giggled again.

He took a trail into the timber, the same trail where April had run that afternoon and Ballard had overtaken her. He held the lantern high as he lurched along, and he found a clearing to one side of the trail and set the lantern down upon a stump and scraped away the fall of dry needles and attacked the ground with the shovel. The dirt was soft and easily worked; the hole grew. Before it got too deep he stepped out of it and surveyed it blearily by the lantern's light. A grave was supposed to be six feet deep, but he couldn't remember how wide or how long it should be. He recalled that Ballard was a tall man, and suddenly he was very sick, but it was not a sickness of his body. He took the quart and drained the last of the whisky in a series of breath-taking gulps. He climbed into the hole and put himself to the task of digging, determined to work too hard to think. He made the dirt fly, and at last he climbed out of the grave, his task done.

Then he turned back toward the house.

And suddenly he was a defeated man. His work with the shovel had brought the sweat, boiling the whisky out of him and leaving him sober. He had planned carefully — the studied drinking in town, the quart to sustain him afterward, the rationing on the ride, but he had not counted on what the work would do to him. He was sober again, sober and sick to the stomach and sick in the mind. Anger grew in him; he should have brought a second quart. Remorse rose and began choking him; he marshaled logic, the careful logic of Ransome Price. He remembered Price's argument about a man going a certain length along a certain trail and not being able to turn back.

He forced himself upon the porch and set the shovel against the wall and moved the lantern to his left hand and opened the door. He held the lantern high; he saw the table and the crude chairs. He stared down at the strips of faded carpet, and Dan Ballard was not there. Only the tangled rope lay there.

He carefully set the lantern upon the table and slumped down into a chair, and surprise gave way to fear, and fear gave way to a strange elation. He was a man who had walked with a shadow a long, long way, and now the shadow was gone. He was sober, but it was a queer sort of sobriety; it left him tired and with tangled thoughts. He wanted to giggle again. He thought of Ransome Price, picturing Price's face as it would look when word reached him that Dan Ballard had escaped. And then Allison laughed.

Later, much later, he lurched through the house to the lean-to. He managed to get one of his boots off, and he fell upon the cot and kicked the tangle of blankets to the floor and lay there; he lay there and it was like being in a hammock; the room swirled slightly, and his stomach tried to betray him, and at long last he slept.

He awoke with his mouth dry and bitter, and the sunlight was strong in the lean-to, and the heat had already taken a hard hold. He sensed dizzily that it was midday; he came out into the kitchen and dipped water from a bucket. It was stale water, tepid and tasteless, but he drank a great deal of it. He went out to the pump for more water and washed his face and thought of food, but the thought was distasteful. He walked into the front room and looked at the rope upon the floor. He sat in a chair and remembered the grave he'd dug, and he put his hands to his face and sobbed dryly, saying, "God! Oh, God!"

He was this way when April opened the door.

He looked up at her and saw the change in her. She still wore the Levis and plaid shirt, and her hair still hung to her shoulders, and she was a wildling, but she was unafraid. Scorn was in her, and she was an adult now and his equal. This drove fear into him. He wanted to run from those eyes; he wanted to hide from them. He could do neither, so he sought refuge in an habitual anger. He said, "Where the hell have you been these last few days? I ought to use a whip on you!"

She said, "You always cut much deeper with words. That's why you never used a whip."

She crossed the room and entered her bedroom; he made no attempt to stop her. He could hear her moving about; bureau drawers opened and closed. She was not gone long. She came back into the front room with a suitcase in her hand; it was an old suitcase, battered and much traveled.

He said, "Where are you going?"

"As far away from you as I can get."

He said, "I'm still your father. I'll stop you," but it sounded rather helpless and futile, even to his own ears.

She said, "You're not my father — not any more. I was here last night. I had two places I could go; I came here because of something a man said to me that made me think."

He gestured toward the rope on the floor. "Him?" he demanded with sudden understanding. "So that's how he got away."

"Yes," she said, "I freed him." Defiance flared in her. "I happen to love him."

Now he had something he could fasten onto; his lip curled and the scorn in his eyes matched hers, and he laughed, and it was not pleasant. He said, "You fell in love with Dan Ballard!

196

You picked a man who's engaged to another woman. But that won't matter, and you'll twist him around your finger. You'll know how to do that, because you're your mother's daughter."

She stepped to the shelf of books and took down a certain engineering book and shook the photograph of her mother from its pages. She looked at the picture for a long moment, and then she tucked it into her pocket. He half rose from the chair; her eyes drove him back.

She said, "Did my mother ever leave a man tied upon a floor? Or did she go out in the woods in the middle of the night and dig a grave? You see, when I came back last night, I went to the hayloft to sleep. I was afraid to come to the house, afraid you might be waiting, afraid of the things you'd lay on me with your foul tongue. I heard you stumbling around in the barn. I followed you when you went with the lantern. I saw what you dug and knew who you were digging it for. And I laughed, knowing he'd got away from you."

His mouth was very dry. "You saw me —" he said.

"That's why I just packed up," she said. "But I waited till you were awake. Before I left, I wanted to tell you why I was going."

He said desperately, "Believe this, April:

I was glad — glad, do you understand — when I found he'd got away! I didn't want to do it. I just hadn't any choice."

She said, "I don't know what deviltry you're mixed into. You've been up to something sneaking ever since we came to this country. It looks like murder would have been part of it. You've lashed at me about my mother. You've told me I'd come to no good end. You got me to believing I was bad. Maybe you were right. Maybe I *am* bad. Maybe you thought it long enough to make it so. But if I'm bad, now I know why. It's because I'm *your* daughter, not because I'm hers. I see now why she must have left you. Maybe you dug another grave, and she knew about it."

He said, "It's not so! It's not so!"

Lifting the suitcase, she crossed to the door and opened it. He knew he should get out of the chair and stop her; he knew, too, that he couldn't stop her, that she was gone from him forever. He knew he had brought this about. He said, "Where are you going?"

"To a man," she said. "No, not to Dan Ballard. He belongs to somebody else. You see, I was in town the day he was supposed to get married. The man I'm going to is the kind that I'm used to — the kind I had for a father — a killer. Maybe I can change him.

Maybe I can do some good for him, and, doing it, do some good for myself. It doesn't matter about me. Not after last night."

He said, "You're getting married." And suddenly his eyes widened. "To Lew Fanshawe. You're the one who got him out of jail. Never mind how I know."

She said, "I could do worse. Remember the taint in my blood you've talked of so many times."

She opened the door and stepped beyond it and closed the door. He still wanted to go after her, but he knew no words to call her back. He heard her footsteps recede, and this was his moment of greatest agony. He thought, *She's mine; she was born of my passion.* He remembered her laughter; there'd been so little of it. He remembered those clippings she'd cut from magazines and pinned upon her bedroom wall. He knew her hunger now and her loneliness; he knew she had lived with a hope and a fear when she'd lived with him, and the hope had been for one kind word, one caress. She'd been within reach always, and he'd shoved her away from him.

And so he sat through that long afternoon, sat and looked back at the parade of the years and let his remorse fester. Sometimes he remembered April and sometimes he remembered his wife, the one becoming the other, and he knew that it all might have been different if he had been different. He went to the dipper for water whenever his thirst grew too great, but always he came back to the chair and sat staring. And so he grew to loathe himself; he looked at himself now as April had looked at him today. He'd been bitter and cynical, a man with no heart in him. But he'd never been crooked, not until he'd come to this Purgatory country. He turned this over in his mind until a new hate came into him. But he couldn't put all the blame onto Price. He hadn't had to listen to Price's proposition when they'd first met, and he hadn't had to listen last night when Price had sent him back here to do murder.

The long, hot day ended; the dusk came creeping, but still he didn't stir. The darkness flowed into the room and turned each object hazy; the heat still held here, more oppressive with the darkness. The hours passed, and he heard hoofbeats in the clearing. His thought was that here was Dan Ballard, returned with the Hourglass crew behind him to demand an accounting; but he refused to care.

Someone knocked at the door. He let the knocking grow more demanding, and then he said, "Come in." A man stood silhouetted in the open doorway; he was a nondescript man, a hanger-on at one of the Ballardton

200

saloons. He said, "Allison?"

Allison nodded.

"I was paid to ride hard and bring this note to you," the man said. He groped forward and laid a sealed envelope on the table. He backed from the room closing the door after him, and the hoofbeats rose again and then receded.

For a long time Allison let the note lie. Then he stirred himself and got a lamp to burning, and he ran his thumb under the flap and shook out the note and read it. It had no salutation, no signature, and even the handwriting was slightly disguised, but it was Ransome Price's.

It said, *I know Ballard got away on you. He was out at the Hourglass today. Don't be worried. Ballard won't count much any longer. The Hourglass turned down the Tomahawk, and Cantrell has gone back to the hills to bring down his cattle and take over the springs. The Hourglass will fight, but it will be a losing fight. The water is as good as ours.*

He read the note and read it again, but never with any real interest. And then a thought took hold of him and grew; he had lived too long with hate to lose his taste for it in a day. But now the hate had turned inward, blighting him, and the hate grew to encompass another; and that other was Ransome Price.

He came to a stand and moved out upon the porch. He remembered April; he remembered her declaring her love for Dan Ballard. He looked in the direction in which the Tomahawk lay. He'd stop them! He'd stop the whole Cantrell outfit all by himself! And then he began walking, his scheme shaping itself. There was this thing he could do for April, but April would never know about it. Therein lay the bitterness, the bitterness and a magnificence beyond measuring.

15

Through the Night

Dan Ballard came through the night; he came at a hard tilt while the flatness was before him, staying with the main trail until it began climbing upward. After the first timber he rode more cautiously, sparing his mount, sparing himself. He could feel the havoc that Mace Cantrell's fists had wrought upon him; his body ached as the riding became harder; and he dismounted then and gave his horse a blow. Afterward he walked, leading the horse behind him. He had to keep himself from stiffening up, he reflected. At least for a day or two. It was here now, the showdown; it was the Hourglass and Tomahawk in a finish fight.

On that high promontory where he'd paused the day before and had his look at the country and remembered Gramp Ballard riding in on a roundabout trail from Texas, he halted again. Night made a difference to the vista; night softened it and made of it a fairyland of silver and purple. He looked back toward the springs; he could see a fire winking, but there was only one fire. Wayne, then, had sent their neighbors home. Remembering the loyalty of the Hashknife and the Circle-Bar and the Wagon Wheel, Dan's throat tightened. If Cantrell took over the springs, they'd take up the club against him, and he wondered then if he'd not made a mistake in not letting the three spreads buy into a fight that might become theirs anyway. But he remembered Gramp saying, "I wish your dad was here to see you tonight, Dan," and he knew now what Gramp had meant. It wasn't the range that counted, or the water; it was whether a Ballard remained a Ballard.

And thinking of this, he remembered Fanshawe, in the cave, speaking of the kind of man who was born to a name and a heritage. He remembered Fanshawe asking, "What did you ever do to earn it, Ballard?" and Dan knew now the real reason why he had spurned his neighbors' help.

He began climbing again, still leading the horse. He could hear the lost voice of the Purgatory; soon he was to where he had looked down upon Clayton Allison. The jutting rock was naked in the moonlight; Dan veered away at this point and found a game trail leading into the timber that flanked the pass road. Mounting, he followed this trail toward the west, glad to be done with openness, glad to be beyond the reach of moonlight. The Cantrells might be expecting the war to be fetched to them. The Cantrells might be posted along the pass road. But they couldn't watch all these back country trails.

Once Dan thought he heard a faraway shout or its thin echo. He listened intently, hoping for a repetition, but there was none. He was getting jumpy, he decided.

The timber pressed around him and the darkness was so thick he felt he might rub it between thumb and forefinger; he felt he might gather a handful of it and stuff it in his pocket. Sometimes, when the canopy of boughs overhead was not so tightly laced, a little moonlight trickled through; it freckled the trail and told him he was keeping to it; but quite often he had to light matches. He was very careful with these. The way was comparatively level now, so he always climbed back upon the horse, keeping low in the saddle, keeping his right arm crooked before his face.

He kept veering steadily westward; somewhere in this direction lay the cave. It had been a good many years since he'd followed a trail to that cave, discounting the blindfolded trip he'd taken yesterday. He tried to remember all the landmarks, and his thoughts grew twisted with the trying. He recalled how he and April had come toiling up that tilting ledge to the cave's mouth and how he had sensed then a picture that tugged at his memory. He had known the cave, of course, when he'd stepped inside it and the blindfold had been whisked away. He had played pirate there as a boy; he'd come with a bandanna wrapped around his head and a sash wrapped around his waist, and he had carried a butcher knife in the sash. He'd stolen that butcher knife from Charley Wong, and Charley had been vociferously angry about it, showing no tolerance for a pirate's need for a cutlass. But Dan had talked of repelling boarders; he had pointed out the need to defend treasure from any who might try to wrest it away from him, and Charley had let him keep the knife.

He smiled now at the remembrance, smiled across the years at the small boy with the bandanna and sash and butcher knife, and then he smiled no more. It had been a grim game then, and it was a grimmer game now. It had the Cantrells mixed into it, and the Allisons, and Lew Fanshawe; and a lot of men could die because of it.

The country was roughening, and he found himself riding the crest of a ridge; he led the horse down into a ravine, crossed over and climbed to the next ridge. He didn't remember this terrain from his childhood days, and he frowned, wondering if he'd veered in the wrong direction. Then he struck another game trail; it led westward, and, a mile along it, he came upon the ruin of a log and shake cabin. Nothing was here now but the shell of what had once been a home to some prospector who had known this country before the Ballards had known it, who had lived here and vanished from the sight and knowledge of men, leaving no name behind him, leaving nothing but this cabin. But Dan remembered the cabin, and, remembering it, he knew he was on the right trail. He wondered if he had passed the cabin blindfolded last night.

Now the underfooting became rockier and the timber thinned out and there was much more moonlight. He grew thirsty; night had banished the plague of heat, and a man might need blankets in this high country before dawn, and this coolness was good, but still he was thirsty. He put his mind from the need. Shortly he crossed what had once been a roaring creek; the gravel was bone dry, and there was not a trickle of water. He damned the drought.

He crossed the creek bed and came into a strip of timber; the darkness closed down and enfolded him again, but he was through the strip quickly, and beyond it lay one of those mountain meadows, grassy and forgotten, where Sam Digby had grazed his cattle. This meadow was a pool of moonlight; across it a man came riding, not pressing his horse but letting it choose its own gait. Dan had never seen this man in a saddle before, but he knew him to be Lew Fanshawe.

Dan drew his own horse back into the deeper shadows at the fringe of the timber; he took his gun from its holster and held it loosely in his hand. He sat thus until Fanshawe was near enough that he could see the solidness of his features, and he rode out then, the gun held ready, and said, "Raise 'em."

Fanshawe's astonishment gave way to recognition and then to anger. He raised his hands and sat with his eyes bleak and half veiled, and his lips skinned back from his teeth. "You play it safe," he said.

Dan reached and plucked Fanshawe's guns one after the other and tossed them aside. He said, "Where is she, Fanshawe?"

One of Fanshawe's eyebrows twitched. "April?"

"Who else?"

Fanshawe shrugged "How should I know? She rode away with *you* last night."

Dan said, "You're running out on her, eh? I don't know that horse you're riding, but I know its brand. It belonged to Sam Digby. Allison must have bought the stock with the place. That must be the horse April rode when she came to Ballardton and got you out of jail. She turned Cantrell's horse loose."

Fanshawe said, "Maybe she *gave* me the jughead. She'd do a thing like that for me. Is that what's eating you?"

Dan said, "Where is she, Fanshawe?"

Fanshawe said, "So you've fallen for her. Fallen hard."

"She needed a friend," Dan said. "I could see that. She saved my life yesterday — twice probably. I came back to make sure no harm came to her. But you wouldn't savvy that."

Fanshawe said, "Then it's her you're looking for, not me. Get out of the way. You're blocking the trail."

Dan thought, *He's making a cat-and-mouse game out of this, that's what he's doing! He hates me and he wants to bedevil me, so he means to tell me nothing.* Anger choked the last patience out of him and he stepped down from his saddle and walked out into the moonlight and reached and got a hard hold on Fanshawe's belt and dragged him from the horse. Dan's jaw tightened, and he said, "Talk, damn you! I've asked you twice where she is!"

Fanshawe's teeth shone white in the moonlight. "Don't work yourself into a lather," he said. "She's at the cave. She didn't show back last night, but she came late today and she fetched her suitcase with her. Her and her old man had some kind of a fight. She came to ride away with me."

209

"But two on one horse made slow traveling, eh?" Dan said. "You didn't want to bother with her. You gave her some kind of story about coming back for her, and then you rode out."

Fanshawe said, "It's getting you, isn't it? About her and me. You don't know what there's been between us, and it's worrying you because you're in love with her. You've been wondering about night before last when we hid out in the cave together. You've been picturing us in the darkness, and it's eating the heart out of you. And I'm laughing because I've got a knife in you and I'm turning it around."

Dan hit him; he struck out wildly with his left fist and Fanshawe saw the blow coming and pulled his head to one side and Dan's knuckles glanced against Fanshawe's ear. It dumped Fanshawe to the ground, that blow; he sat there staring up at Dan, and hate was naked in Fanshawe's eyes. He said, "You've got the guts when you've got a gun in your hand."

Dan droppd the gun into his holster and reached and hauled Fanshawe to a stand and kept his hand wrapped in Fanshawe's shirt front. Dan said, "Talk now, or start swinging your fists. I haven't got time to fool around."

They were this way for a moment, toe to

toe and eye to eye, and the hate was still in Fanshawe, but the fear crept into him, too, and showed in his face. He said, "I might have taken her with me, but she held out for a wedding ring. That's when I walked out. She'd have been good company for a week or a month, but why the hell should I have saddled myself with her? Besides, she wasn't going to ride away with me for her own sake, she was going to do it for mine. I never could abide a reforming woman."

Dan said, "Is that all of it?"

The hate flared upward and consumed Fanshawe. "No, damn you! I could have treated her like a squaw if it hadn't been for you. She was crazy enough about me to bust me out of jail, but she saw you while she was doing it. That changed everything for her. I knew it night before last in the cave, but I couldn't show her who was boss. I needed her to steal grub from her old man. Maybe I should have took her along, even if it meant a wedding ring. Maybe I should have done that just for the sake of beating you."

Dan hit him again. Fanshawe went down, and Dan reached for him once more and hauled him to his feet. Dan said, "I owed you one for that clout you gave me in the jail building. That one just now was for her."

Fanshawe's voice turned deadly. "I never

was handy with my fists. And you're still the man with the gun."

Dan crossed to where the moonlight danced on one of the guns he'd taken from Fanshawe and tossed away. He picked up this gun and walked back and thrust it hard into Fanshawe's holster. He stepped backward a dozen paces from Fanshawe and said, "Now, damn you!"

They stood this way, looking at each other across the moon-silvered distance. They stood there, and Dan was remembering the sun-drenched street of Ballardton, and Fanshawe under the wooden awning of the Rialto, and the silence, and the first betraying flicker of Fanshawe's eyes. He thought, *Here we go again!* and there was no fear in him; he had bested this man once and he knew he could best him again. He looked at Fanshawe and waited — and he saw Fanshawe die. Not with a bullet in him; there was no play at guns. He saw the heart die in Fanshawe and the courage of Fanshawe shrivel, and Fanshawe said then, hoarsely, "To hell with you!" but there was no iron in it, it was only a quavering cry.

Dan strode toward him; Fanshawe stood waiting, watching Dan with eyes that were afraid. Fanshawe said, "What are you going to do?"

Dan said, "Last night I would have settled to let you ride out of the country. But you're a Cantrell man; you proved that when you planned to keep me in the cave until after the Cantrell deadline. The war's on, Fanshawe. Now I'm going to make sure of one less gun against the Hourglass. There's a cabin back a piece. I'm taking you there and tying you while I go on to the cave. When I come back, I'm collecting you to turn you over to Abe Potter."

The blood drained out of Fanshawe's face and he was something craven, sickening to look upon. He said, "You'll leave me tied up for hours? With a fire eating through the hills?"

"Fire!" Dan ejaculated.

Fanshawe swept his arm to the northeast. "It's back there. Can't you hear it? Or smell it? Some fool with a cigarette, I suppose. There's no wind and it isn't heading this way, but it might. You can't leave me tied up in this timber country! You can't do it!"

Dan said, *"Shhh —"* and paused, listening, his ears strained. He heard it then, the distant crackle; it was miles away and it wasn't much of a fire, not yet. There was no wind; a wind could spread the fire fast. He listened and horror rose in him and choked him and he crossed quickly to his horse and heaved himself into

213

the saddle He glared down at Fanshawe, and he said, "And you rode out and left her afoot in the hills with a forest fire burning! I ought to kill you. But I can't force a fight on you. And I can't shoot you down. Once a man made the remark that you were nothing one way or the other. He was right!"

He wheeled the horse and headed it at a hard gallop across the meadow. In this manner he put his back to Fanshawe, and Fanshawe had a loaded gun, but there was no concern in Dan. Not about this. Fanshawe might like to shoot him in the back, but the man would be afraid to try. He'd be afraid Dan would be expecting such a play — hoping for it. And then he forgot Fanshawe, remembering only the cave and the girl alone, and the flaming beast that had been unleashed in the hills.

16

Forest Aflame

At first, to Dan, the thought with terror in it — the thought of April back yonder in the cave with the fire sweeping through the hills to entrap her — was like a lash laid upon him. But, once he was across the meadow and onto a timber-fringed trail, he put down this fear, knowing it could numb a man, knowing it could make his judgment uncertain. He mustn't let himself be stampeded. He mustn't let this panic him. He marshaled logic, but all the while he was still forcing the horse with the recklessness of desperation.

It couldn't be much of a fire. He told himself that over and over again. If the fire had had a real start, he'd have seen the glow of it while he was still down on the flats. That fire had got started only recently, and maybe it was in some isolated gulch and would burn itself out. He looked aloft to the pine tops prayerfully, there was no wind to speak of. He could hear the distant sound of the fire, the insidious crackling that spoke of a slow eating of trees and underbrush; he fancied he could smell the smoke. He tried to determine the exact location of the fire; he gave this up as fruitless.

He mastered himself, besting the fear; he mastered the horse, pulling it down to a walk. But the fire was still there, in the hills, in his consciousness.

"Some fool with a cigarette," Fanshawe had guessed. Dan wondered about that; hill people knew the dryness of the woods; hill people would have been mighty careful. And there's been no storm, no lightning, to have set the forest aflame. A man-made fire, set with deliberation? He thought of the Cantrells; had they expected the war would be carried to them and thus started the fire to rear the barrier of it between the Tomahawk and any invaders? He discounted this at once; the Cantrells couldn't run such a risk, not when their cattle grazed back here and a rising wind could make of the fire a Frankenstein's monster. He thought of Fanshawe, who had known of the fire and said nothing until his own skin was in jeopardy. Fanshawe had that kind of poison in him; Fanshawe would not have been above setting a fire. But for what purpose? Let the wind rise and Fanshawe might die in these hills even yet.

Clayton Allison crept into his consideration; Allison drew a poor man's living from the wooded acres that had been Sam Digby's, and Allison's holdings might be wiped out before the night was through. He thought of Allison and feared for the man, but it never seriously crossed his mind that Allison might have set the fire. There was a madness in Allison, but it wasn't that kind of madness; the man was no witless vandal; the man had intelligence and would have been thoughtful of his own skin.

Below, on the flats where the Hourglass kept vigil at Ballard Springs, they'd be seeing the glow against the sky. They'd know that for what it portended; they would be remembering that Dan Ballard was up here somewhere, and they would be afraid. Perhaps some of them would come riding in search of him — Wayne, or Barney Partridge. A thought struck Dan. Had the Cantrells set the fire hoping to draw the Hourglass into the hills, away from the springs? But there were too many ragged edges to that kind of reasoning. The Tomahawk had not yet had time to gather its cattle; the Cantrells would want their herd bunched and beyond the fireline before planning such a coup. And where would the Cantrells have found assurance that a fire would draw the Hourglass into the hills? They hadn't known that Dan Ballard would be riding the high country tonight.

So thinking, he came upon the fire.

He had been aware that the sound of the fire was much nearer; he had been aware of smoke. Now the trail topped a ridge to parallel its crest, and, humping over the rise, he found a wooded gorge below him, running east and west, and in this gorge was smoky chaos, with the white ash slowly rising and hanging listlessly in the air. The fire was a ground-hogging monster, a creeping thing, showing its red teeth intermittently. Sometimes it reared upward with startling force, wrapping itself around the base of a tree, setting a bush blazing vividly. The heat rose and smote Dan; the low, ominous roar was steady in his ears; the smoke made him weep. His horse became fractious, snorting and sidestepping, and it took all his power to hold the mount to the trail. He glanced back, trying to gauge the extent of the fire; it seemed to follow the gulch's contours. This would fix the Cantrells, he reflected; they couldn't get through now until the fire burned itself out. But there was no consolation in that.

He began to sweat; the sweat drenched him and plastered his shirt to him, and cinders landed on his clothes, and once he had to beat out a spark. The smell of smoldering flannel stayed with him, but the smoke was the worst thing; it got at his throat; it blinded his eyes. He looked to the left, down into another gorge, and wondered if he could lead the horse there. He decided to stay with the ridge, and soon he came to its end and dropped down to level country, and now he was skirting the fire and could look into the heart of it. If only it didn't crown! He had seen a crown fire once; he remembered the flames writhing upward to the tree tops, leaping from tree to tree, spreading with devastating rapidity. Now he was a man pacing a tractable lion which kept its distance and offered him no real harm but which could suddenly turn upon him and become many lions, surrounding him.

A deer broke out of the brush not half-a-horse ahead of him. It stood for a moment, frozen in its panic, the fire reflected in its eyes, and then it was gone, running into the far brush. The horse tried again to bolt; he supposed he'd have to blindfold the beast. The air grew stifling; the heat pressed down and was relentless and ponderous and almost tangible. The mount's panic became a contagion; for a moment terror swept over Dan, and his impulse was to turn and find another trail and put himself as far from the fire as possible. He remembered the deer. Those animals knew!

He wondered how far he was from the cave; nothing was familiar any more; there were no landmarks; there were only heat and smoke and the lurid flames to his right, and the drifting ash in the air. He fought a new panic, fearful that he was going in the wrong direction. The smoke brought on a fit of coughing, and he reeled in the saddle, clutching at the horn, and almost lost control of the horse. The ground became rocky underfoot; he saw a high, dark outline ahead. Relief swept through Dan. The cave was inside that hill, and on the far side of the hill he would find the trail that climbed the ledge to the cave's mouth.

He went forward blindly through swirling smoke. He kept a steady hand on the reins, but he let the horse pick its own way. Skirting the hill, he put the rise of earth between himself and the fire, and thereafter he was in darkness again. When he was able to peer upward and dimly discern the cave, he dismounted, glancing about in search of a bush stout enough to anchor the frightened horse. He found one and wrapped the reins around the stalk and stumbled to the ledge and began climbing it. It had been easier going when he'd made the ascent blindfolded. The smoke was seeping around the hill; the smoke was here. He looked down upon brush and stunted trees. If the fire crept around and set all that ablaze, what then?

He got to the cave's mouth and stumbled inside. No fire burned in here as there'd been when April had fetched him to the place;

blackness enveloped him. He cried out hoarsely, *"April?"* And only then did he allow himself to think that perhaps she wasn't here, perhaps she had dared the woods and been trapped between the cave and Digby's place. Horror made him lightheaded and took the strength out of him, and he thought for a moment that his knees would not sustain him. Then there was rustling movement to the rear of the cave and she came groping toward him, her hand reaching out and touching his arm.

"Dan!" she said.

He leaned against her, his arms fumbling for her. "Oh, God!" he said.

"I tried to go home," she said. "The fire had me cut off. I came back here. I've been lying with my face to the floor."

He could smell the smoke; it had crept into the cave to writhe in the darkness. He said, "I've got a horse." He took her by the wrist and groped toward the entrance and got out upon the ledge. He was careful on the descent; the smoke had become a pall, blotting out the stars. He set one foot ahead of the other and tested each step before he took it. He got to the bottom of the ledge and moved to where he'd left the horse, and the horse was gone. Falling to his knees, his eyes smarting, he groped with his hands and found where the bush had been pulled up by the roots. He said dismally, "He got panicked and bolted." This was the worst moment for him.

She said, "Shall we go back to the cave?"

His first impulse was to say yes. He looked about him; the fire had crept around the north side of the hill and flowed into the levels; a juniper suddenly became a torch; it stood out starkly for a moment and then was a blackened nothing. He thought how it would be in the cave, hugging the floor, feeling the heat and fighting the smoke, gasping for air and making that vain fight until they had no strength to fight any longer, and suffocation came. He said, "No!" and it was a shout. Odd how curiously hard it was to make yourself heard in this lowering atmosphere.

He got her by the wrist again and they went running and stumbling to the south. The fire came creeping that way, too, around the base of the hill. A burning brand arced through the air; another followed it. Flame roared up a pitch-covered tree trunk and a lofty hemlock became a pillar of flame. The fire spanned itself from this tree to another, and Dan sensed then that there was a wind. *God!* he thought, *it's crowning!* He went running hard, dragging April along beside him. They got beyond this section of timber and began clawing their way up a ridge. Atop its crest they paused, looking upon the spreading inferno behind them;

snapping branches were like a barrage of rifle fire. Then they dropped over the ridge and went stumbling and groping downward, into timber, into weird darkness.

They found a trail; it led eastward and they followed it. That was all the planning there was left in Dan, to head east or south. Either way led out of the timber. They ran until they could run no more. They paused, sobbing for breath; they felt the heat and saw the fireglow bloodying the sky; and this ravine was like a horizontal chimney, sucking the hot wind.

"It's here," April said. "It jumped the ridge."

Dan said hoarsely, "Damn it! Damn the fire!"

It was going to get him; he knew that now. It was wily, that fire; it was a monster playing a stalking game with him, making him run till his lungs burst, making him hope for safety when there was no safety. It was made of dryness and madness; it was the drought taking a tangible form. It was all the rainless days concentrated into a blazing club that would beat him down. It had long ago gotten Old Man Cantrell; it had dried up Cantrell's mountain creeks and turned the man's selfishness into a lust for Hourglass's water. It had worked on Wayne, too, shriveling the courage in Wayne and turning him old before his time.

It had even changed Cynthia, making her a stranger to the man she was to have married. But Dan had stood impervious to the drought; he had laughed at it and told the others that a little rain would wash away their madness. But the drought had bided its time; it had contemplated this puny mortal who derided it, and it had laughed its dry, silent laughter — and waited. And now it had him trapped.

April said, "What did you say?"

Only then did he realize he'd been talking aloud. He dragged his sleeve across his face; he dashed away the perspiration and swept some of the madness from him with it. He said, "We'll have to run for it again."

In the eerie, flickering light he looked at her, seeing the black soot upon her face. He looked at her and smiled, then reached for her hand and led her along the trail until the trail petered out and they found themselves in the maze of an old windfall. Now they had to climb over ancient logs that sometimes were piled high and criss-crossed like jackstraws; he gave her his hand when he could. He'd better go easy here, he reflected, or he'd break a leg. The heat was upon them and the roar of the fire was in their ears and the smoke had them both weeping and choking, and he wondered just when the enemy would burst into the windfall and surround them. His desperation whetted, he grew careless of risk. At least the fire put a light in here, and that helped. Progress was painfully slow. It was a matter of climbing and crawling and clawing along; it was like moving in a nightmare, expending effort and sweating, yet seeming to get nowhere.

Brands had been sailing overhead; now they began dropping in here. The tangle of logs was thinning out; Dan looked back and found April toiling behind him. He said, "Here," and gave her his hand, and then they were stumbling into a gravelly creek bottom. There was a trickle of water, and Dan came down to his knees and sucked at it and loosened his bandanna and soaked it and mopped his face. April had a drink; she lay prone and exhausted and might have stayed here except that he dragged at her and got her beyond the creek and went stumbling into the brush. It took forever to find a trail, but the trail led eastward. He could still cling to that one need — move east or south! But the fire seemed to be on two sides of them now, and behind them, and it was moving faster than a galloping horse. The smoke strangled Dan and was like thumbs gouging at his eyes; the smoke made a swirling haze through which they groped blindly. Dan was afraid he might go unconscious; he wondered how that would be, just dropping down and giving up the effort and letting the drought win.

He said, "Do you know where we are?" He shouted it.

April shook her head.

He pressed onward; the woods grew light as day, and the trail wound ever eastward. A steer came lumbering out of a thicket; it charged wild-eyed and almost bowled them over in passing; it crashed into the brush opposite the trail and was gone. It had worn the Tomahawk brand; Dan had seen it in the lurid, unearthly light. He thought of his bolted horse and hoped the horse had won through to safety.

Then he and April were stumbling out upon a road, and there was no sense to that until Dan suddenly realized it was the Tomahawk Pass road. Just beyond was the gorge; he hadn't heard the rumble of the Purgatory because the roar of the fire was in his ears. Across there was safety, and his eyes spanned the gorge in futile hope. But at least he knew now where he was. He went lurching down the road, April beside him; he reached and took her hand again. If they just kept going this way, they were bound to reach the flats, he reasoned. But now, through the wall of timber flanking the road, he could see the fire; brands sailed out here and fell upon the road or spanned the river to drop upon the far side of the gorge. Dan's desperation grew. They'd almost won through, and now they were to be trapped!

The fire rode high and the fire crept low. The massing pines beside the road had ceased to stand starkly silhouetted against the fire behind them; the fire had reached the road and turned the timber into torches. The brands fell more thickly and April pressed close to him, saying nothing, but he felt the fear in her. They moved to the far side of the road and the danger was that a mis-step might send them plunging into the chasm.

Then Dan saw the jutting rock ahead, the rock that thrust outward like a thumb over the edge of this near wall. He reached the rock and moved out upon it; he wondered if they could make a stand here. But he knew the burning brands would get them, or the heat and the smoke. He could see the road below; the fire was already down there; a tree exploded and fell blazing across the road. He looked at April and said, "Can you swim?"

She nodded.

He drew her close to him; he didn't want to have to shout; his throat was raw. He looked at her, and all the questions he'd wanted to ask came crowding, but he never voiced them. She'd come to some sort of decision tonight, he knew; she'd tried to make a bargain with Lew Fanshawe, but it had had to be a certain kind of bargain. He remembered now that she hadn't been surprised when he, Dan, had appeared at the cave; she hadn't asked him why he'd come. He shook these things from his head; this was not the time for talk.

He said, "We've got one chance. The river is below, but it's a mighty long drop. We're below the rapids, and there's a pool straight down. It always looked like a deep pool. If we jump from here, maybe we can swim on south to safety. It's a long chance, but a better one than we'll have if we stay here and let the fire close in on us, or if we try to break through it. What do you say?"

Her face was oily with perspiration and streaked with soot; her face was calm. "I'd rather drown than burn."

He looked toward that wall of fire, and, looking, shuddered. Brands fell around them and one touched his shoulder and he patted frantically at the smoldering flannel. The light washed the far wall of the gorge; it painted the rock vividly, but it didn't show down into the black depths. He stripped off his gun belt and let it drop. He seated himself and tugged at his boots, and April did likewise and succeeded in removing her own. His own refused to budge, even when she lent him a hand; his feet were too swollen from walking, and he gave up the effort. He came to a stand and stepped toward the edge of the rock and smiled at her and said, "Are you afraid?"

She took his hand. "Not with you."

There was no need for waiting, no sense in it. Waiting might drain the courage out of them. He said, "Here goes," and his fingers tightened on hers, and they stepped out into space together. Only then did he hear the voice of the river.

17

The Tomahawk Strikes

Terror rises in a man on a long, plummeting drop through space; it takes the stomach out of him and fills him with a sick dread; and it was thus with Dan. He knew the pool was directly below, the silent, dark pool, but he remembered how shallow the Purgatory had looked yesterday. Supposing the pool was only a few feet deep now! He knew that striking the water would be like striking a wall if he hit awkwardly. He struggled in midair, keeping himself straight, and he struck feet first, April striking with him. The impact was savage; it drove the wind from Dan and he went far beneath the surface, and he was conscious then of the coolness of the water and the smothering pressure of it, conscious of that and the fact that he'd lost his grip on April.

Panic had its way with him, and he fought it down, clawing blindly and fighting toward the surface. It took forever before he felt air against his face and sucked it in. He called, *"April!"* frantically, desperately. The roar of the rapids was in his ears; the fire-lighted sky high above wheeled wildly; the canyon walls became a rushing darkness. The current had him and was sweeping him downstream. He stroked along; it was instinct to keep his arms and legs moving. Something smashed out of the darkness, grating against his ribs. His hands flailed out, his arms wrapped around the trunk of an uprooted tree that had been plucked from the higher hills and sent hurtling downstream. He clung hard and rode with the tree.

His worry was for April; he strained his eyes against the spray-filled darkness and called her name, knowing how futile it was to try to out-shout the rapids. An undertow seized him and sucked him beneath the surface, tree and all; he lost his grip on the tree and struggled to break water, and when he did he was close to the west wall of the canyon. Ahead and to his right loomed a rock; he set his eyes on this rock and paddled wearily toward it, sobbing with exertion. The rock seemed to recede from him until a wild, patternless eddy swept him at it. He was going to hit hard, he realized, but there was no strength in him to prepare for the impact. He caromed against the rock and reached out and clutched for it; water-polished sandstone slid under his claw-ing fingers, but he got his hold. It was then he found April. She was here, too, holding fast to the rock; her face a white, strained glimmer in the darkness.

He shouted at her; he wasn't sure he made himself heard. He cried, "Let's try for the west wall!" He knew they couldn't remain here; he knew the river's tearing hands would pull them away when their strength was spent and send them hurtling with the current. He could see the wall; it loomed tantalizingly close; it was a million miles away. He let go and struck out diagonally toward the wall; April did the same. He got to her and tried to lend her a hand; he found that this wasn't necessary. It came to him as something of a surprise that she was a better swimmer than he.

He lost her again in the darkness; under the overhang of the wall there was no reflected light from the lurid sky above. He felt his knees grate against sandstone; he reached out and found a rough grip on a stub of rock and hauled himself upward. A hand reached to help him, and he half-lifted himself and was half-pulled to one of those ledges that broke the smoothness of the canyon's wall. Spray dampened the ledge; the surface was hard and rough, and he sprawled spent and shaking, sucking in air in great, gasping sobs. He found April beside him, and they lay like this, and he wondered then what wisdom there'd been in choosing the river to the blazing forest. This was just the reverse of the old saying. This was out of the fire and into the frying pan.

He lay for a long time, not trying to talk. He felt the strength come back into his limbs, but his body ached. He'd been taking too many beatings of one kind and another lately, he decided. He sat up, and April did likewise, crowding closer to him. He felt her shiver and he put his arm around her and his lips close to her ear and said, "It was quite a ride, wasn't it?"

She nodded, and he said, "Possibly we could work our way along these ledges, but it will be pretty risky without daylight." He left her and edged cautiously along on hands and knees, patting carefully ahead of him before he put his weight down. He crept back and said, "This one seems to peter out. We're going to have to have help to get off here. Do you want to try the river again?"

She shuddered. "I'm a good swimmer while I last, but I can't keep it up long."

He said, "If we wait, the Hourglass will come looking for me once the fire burns out. They might be able to make it along the rim by daylight; they might not be able to get anywhere near here for a week. It will depend on the fire. And they'll look in the woods for me, not in the river. There's only one thing to do. I'm going on downstream and try to get to our crew. Then I can lead them to you."

She crept close to him; she crept into his arms. She said, "Don't go!" and she was a little child, terrified at being alone. She was quiet for a long time; he held her close, trying to comfort her, wondering how to comfort her. She said then, "You'll have to go, of course. I'll wait until noon tomorrow. If you're not back by then, I'll try the river before I get too weak from hunger."

He said, "Good girl!" He tried tugging at his boots; they still resisted him. He took her in his arms again and kissed her, and he said, "So long," trying to make it sound cheerful. He said, "Here goes nothing," and let himself off the ledge and into the water. The current caught him, swirling him away; he had one last glimpse of the white blob that was her face, and then it was lost to his sight.

This time he tried no fighting; he let the current sweep him along and he worked only at keeping above water. To conserve his strength, he played a game with the river; he was going to outwit the river. Sometimes floating trees swished past him; twice he was dashed against rocks and clung to them, getting his breath, getting his strength. Each time he let go reluctantly, wanting to stay fast, but knowing that disaster lurked in the notion. The walls still rose above him, but the night sky was no longer fire-lighted, and he knew he must be below the timber. The walls grew farther apart and the current lost its racing buoyancy, and after an interminable time he paddled awkwardly toward the west wall and found a shore here, wide and sloping upward. He pulled himself to the shore and lay for a long time just resting.

He was far below the gorge. He knew this when he began feeling his way along the wall; it was not so precipitous; it was broken in many places, and he clambered into one of these fissures and found stunted bushes growing from its sides, and he began clambering with the help of these. Sometimes he slipped; once he rolled a dozen yards, but there was no sheer drop, no real danger. The last lap was the hardest; the rim was a sandy cutbank, and he had to dig handfalls into it and struggle to make the ascent. He might have explored and found an easier way, but this near to the top he grew impatient. At long last he pulled himself over the rim and lay upon the prairie with the stars wheeling above and the hills off to the north of him, so many miles away that he was astonished at the distance he had covered.

When he had rested, he began walking. Ballard Springs should lie about due west, the way he calculated it, and only a couple of miles away; but the darkness before dawn had closed down upon the land, and he could only go by guesswork. The fire still raged in the hills; a heavy pall of smoke hung yonder and the sky was red as from weeping, and he could orient himself by that ghastly sight. His feet pained him; riding boots were not made for walking, and his were soggy from the river. He was limping badly at the end of the first mile; he was going on sheer will after that. He wanted more than anything in the world to lie down. He remembered April and kept moving.

He was a little feverish and talking to himself when he made out the blotched darkness against darkness ahead of him and identified it as the chuck wagon. He heard the voices, and the movement of horses, and realized dazedly that they'd let the fire go out. He'd counted on there being a fire; he'd intended to follow it as a beacon and bring himself to the Hourglass camp at the springs, and then he'd forgotten about it. He lurched forward, stumbling, trying to run. Someone said coldly, "Just stand your hand and sing out!" He saw a man shape up ahead of him, and he babbled, "It's me! Dan!" and pitched forward on his face.

He heard the rising voices around him; he could sense the excitement in the voices without getting any coherence out of the words.

He felt himself lifted; many hands were at that task. Wayne's voice reached him. Wayne cried, "Dan! Dan!" over and over again in a shaky manner. Wayne sounded as though he were close to blubbering.

Gramp said, "Stretch him out on a blanket, you confounded idiots! Can't you see he's done in?" Gramp's voice reached into Dan, clearing the fog from his mind.

Dan said, "Wayne! Didn't you send him home?"

Wayne said, "He wouldn't go. He just wouldn't go."

Dan felt himself being lowered, and a blanket was beneath him. He said, "If somebody wants to do me the biggest favor in the world, get those damn' boots off!"

They obliged him; he tried wiggling his toes, and they wriggled, and that seemed an important accomplishment. Wayne said, "What in hell happened to you? Long after you'd left, we saw the fire. Then your horse came bolting toward the Hourglass. Barney rode up toward the hills then, to try to find you. He ran into the Cantrells. They must have seen the fire, too, and got through while they could. They're somewhere on the lower pass road. They turned Barney back with bullets."

Dan said, "Here it is — all of it," and he

talked then, lying still upon the blanket and letting the words run. He told of his first trip to the hills, and of Clayton Allison and April and Lew Fanshawe. He told of the urge that had taken him back tonight; he told of the fire and those hideous hours of outrunning it, then of the leap into the river and the decision to risk the current a second time. He struggled to a sitting position when he was through, and he said, "We've got to get back to her! Don't you understand? She's there alone, on the ledge!"

Wayne's hands pressed him down. Wayne said gently, "We can't ride up there without running into the Cantrells. Barney ran into only part of the outfit — the old man and three of the boys. They must have been waiting for the others to get through. When they're all together, they're going to strike at us, sure as shooting. We've got a war to fight before we can reach the gorge."

"Then we'll carry the fight to them!" Dan babbled.

Wayne said, "You couldn't possibly find her until full daylight; you know that. You've got to rest. Can't you get that through your head? You've got to rest!"

Wayne was right, Dan decided. He was holding onto the feathery edge of nothing. He let himself go back upon the blanket; he let himself relax, and the need for rest flowed over him and engulfed him, and for a long while he was conscious of the muted murmur of voices around him, and then he slept. He slept until daylight beat upon his eyes, but even then he might not have awakened except for the pressure of Wayne's hand upon his shoulder. Opening his eyes and looking up, he saw the sky overcast by a gray pall with the sun floating behind this hazy curtain, red and fuzzy. He saw Wayne's thin, drawn face, but he saw a peace in Wayne now, a placidity.

"Time to get up, Dan. The Cantrells are coming."

Wayne said it so quietly that it took a full moment for the import of it to reach into Dan. He sat up on the blanket; he felt reinvigorated, he felt ready to cope with the world. He looked again at Wayne who crouched beside him; Wayne had a gun belt latched about his middle.

Dan said, "Rustle me a spare gun, will you, Wayne? I left mine up at the pass." Wayne nodded and walked toward the chuck wagon, and Dan glanced about him for his boots, but he couldn't find them.

Someone said, "Look at 'em come!"

Dan lifted his eyes to the north, and there, across the flat expanse, a knot of riders came sweeping through the sage, rising and falling, bobbing ever nearer. They came with no thunder to them but the thunder of hoofs, and then, the distance shortened to six-shooter range, they began a wild shouting and a ragged firing; guns were in their hands and smoke came from those guns; a bullet pinged into the canvas tilts of the chuck wagon, a horse squealed in pain. An Hourglass rider, standing not far from Dan's blanket, half turned, his hand clasping against his ribs. He brought his hand away, and there was blood on his fingers; he stared at this in shocked surprise.

This was it, Dan thought. This was really it!

Pandemonium took hold of the Hourglass, but there was little panic in it. Men were running to horses which had been saddled in anticipation of this moment. Men knelt behind the wheels of the chuck wagon and rested rifles on the spokes and made those rifles talk. Charley Wong took a frying pan and began beating upon it with a ladle, hopping about in a frenzy of excitement as he did so. What was the matter with Charley, Dan wondered. Was that the way they made war in China?

Wayne came running back and pressed a gun and belt into Dan's hands. Dan flung the belt about his middle and caught the end and latched it, feeling detached from all this, feeling very much a part of it.

Gramp cried, "Somebody help me up into a saddle, damn it!" Someone boosted him, and he was ahorse. So was Wayne. Dan saw a mount rearing with trailing reins, gun-shy and ready to bolt. He got into the saddle and got the gun into his hand and wheeled the horse, facing north; and the Cantrells were almost upon them.

They were attacking just like Indians, Dan reflected, waiting for daylight and coming with a whoop and a holler. They were showing no more sense than a bunch of Sioux! Then he realized there was no choice for the Cantrells; if they brought a war they had to bring it in this fashion. Sage offered little shelter; the open sweep of land lent itself to no strategy, no cunning. It was roar up a-shooting; it was make this bold play and chance the odds and win or lose on the one throw.

There were nine of them. That would be the old man — you could tell him by the beard — and his five sons, and three riders who drew Tomahawk pay and gave the Tomahawk allegiance. Dan remembered Lew Fanshawe, and his certainty that Fanshawe was a Cantrell man, and he looked for the gunhawk, but Fanshawe was not here. Nine — There were ten in the Hourglass bunch, but that was counting Charley Wong, and that was counting Gramp.

241

Dan looked for Gramp. Gramp was kneeing his horse out front; Gramp had a rifle to his cheek, and his snowy hair flew in the wind, and the rifle made its sullen sound, and a Tomahawk rider threw up his hands and fell backward from his horse. Gramp had been right! There'd been this one last fight left in him, and he'd known it! A bullet plucked at Dan's sleeve; he beat against the horse with his stockinged heels and charged forward with Hourglass riders flanking him. Hourglass and Tomahawk came together and there was the shock of horses striking against horses; there were shouts and curses, and powder smoke in the air, and pains and death, and the sullen sky overhead, and the contested water behind them. Dan saw Wayne. Wayne had crashed against one of Cantrell's boys; Wayne was driving at this one with a gun barrel, knocking him from his horse. Wayne's face was a fighting man's face; it was their father's face. Dan thought, *I hope Gramp sees him! I hope Gramp sees him!*

Dan was into the thick of it himself. Out of the boiling dust he saw a rider loom close by; he saw the man's contorted face and recognized him as Mace Cantrell. He felt a kindliness toward Mace; he had fought Mace one way and bested him, but that had earned him Mace's hate. Mace struck at him with a gun barrel; Dan swerved sideways in the saddle, feeling the blow along his shoulders. He brought up his own gun and clouted at Mace and missed him. Mace triggered; the flame exploded in Dan's face, the powder scorched his cheek, and he heard the whisper of the bullet. He fired then, blindly and without aim, and knew that he'd missed. An Hourglass rider near by lifted his gun, and the thunder of it was a roar in Dan's ear, and Mace seemed to dissolve before him and was gone down into the dust.

After that, the fight was a whirling maelstrom without sense or pattern, where a man went shooting and clouting and looked twice to tell friend from foe. It wasn't a fight; it was a roar in the ears. It was brief, and it was endless, and it was suddenly over when the Tomahawk broke and the remnants went tailing it to the north. Dan drew hard upon his reins then, fighting his horse to a stand, and he looked around him in the settling dust and there were men upon the prairie, some stirring and some not. He looked for Wayne; Wayne was in a saddle, his face powder-scorched, his face triumphant. He looked for Gramp and found him kneeling beside a fallen giant whose rigid beard was pointed to the sky.

Dan got out of the saddle and lurched over

to where Gramp was, and Old Man Cantrell looked up from where he lay and said very plainly, "Damn you! Damn all of you!" and, saying it, died.

Gramp said softly, "I got him. I got him, Daniel. I guess I knew from the first day he came to the hills, so long, long ago, that some day it would end like this."

He looked old and tired; he glanced toward the south. "I want to go home," he said.

Dan looked down upon Old Man Cantrell, seeing the blood upon him, seeing the sightless, staring eyes, and he was suddenly sick. A bullet had done this — a bullet you could hide in your watch pocket or hold in the palm of your hand. A little bit of lead, and this was the end to Cantrell's scheming and his selfishness. And, thinking of this, Dan remembered Gramp's ancient belief that Hourglass calves had gone into the Tomahawk's gathers; he remembered Cantrell's arrogant deadline and Cantrell's ruthless challenge about taking over the springs by force, and he knew that Gramp had been right, always, and that there could have been no other ending.

Wayne came limping up, blood upon his trouser leg. To Dan's quick show of concern, Wayne shook his head. "Only a scratch," he said.

Dan smiled and said, "You did yourself

proud today, Wayne."

Wayne said very solemnly, "Because of you, kid. Because of your kind of guts. Or maybe it was because of Gramp — him and his insisting that he be in on the fight."

Gramp looked up at him and grinned. "I should have used my cane on you as well as on Dan."

Dan looked across the prairie; far to the north the Tomahawk riders were still fleeing. He said, "What's the tally, Wayne?"

Wayne said, "The old man and Mace and Hob and Rufe got it. The other two boys and the hired hands didn't have enough stomach to keep going after that. They've lost face on this range forever, and I'd guess that the fire wiped out their ranch."

"And the Hourglass?"

Wayne's face stiffened. "Pete's dead," he said. "Three other fellows besides myself got nicked. We'll give Doc Church a busy afternoon."

Barney Partridge came bow-legging up; it occurred to Dan that he hadn't glimpsed Barney in the fighting, yet the marks of battle were upon Barney — a smudge of gun powder on one cheek, a cut over one eye — and he wore them proudly. Dan grinned, raising a hand to Barney's shoulder, and he said, "Wayne will have to be getting to Doc Church and taking the other boys along. The rest can see that Gramp gets to the ranch, once the burying is done. Me, I'm riding north again. You can do me a favor, Barney, if you'll rustle up every lariat around the camp."

"I'll do that," Partridge said "And I'll ride with you. You've been doing too much riding alone lately." He grinned and spat. "You can put your boots on now, Daniel. The fight's over and there's no chance of your dying. The Hourglass rules this range from here on out."

18

One More Ride to Make

They toiled toward the pass, the two of them, riding single file beneath the bleak sky with the sun beating pitilessly through the haze, and the heat intensified by that low, gray curtain. They rode warily, remembering that the fleeing remnants of the Tomahawk had bolted in this northerly direction, though Barney Partridge had shown no real concern about the enemy.

"There's a last fight for every man," he'd told Dan when they'd been stirrup to stirrup on the flats. "Your gramp had his today. But he won his fight, so he'll sun himself on the gallery the rest of his days and remember. The Cantrells lost theirs. They'll want no more of this range, and it will be a long time before they'll lift a gun in anger again. They got a bellyful, Daniel."

Dan had nodded. What did he care about the Cantrells? He was remembering April on the ledge. He was remembering that she meant to dare the current if he wasn't back to her by noon.

Where Tomahawk Pass tilted upward they came into the first of the forest; the fire had swept on to the west, leaving a dead and blackened stand of skeleton timber in its wake, leaving desolation. The ash was knee-deep; the ash stirred to the breeze and raised a ghostly mist; no bird sang, no cricket chirped, no life showed itself. Dan looked and shuddered, seeing a nightmare land. Partridge said mournfully, "All that timber shot to hell an' gone." Higher in the hills the black pall blotted out the peaks; yonder, miles away, the fire still raged.

The road was passable; sometimes, though, when they began skirting the gorge they came to where a tree had fallen in blazing ruin across the road and burned itself out. Most of these they were able to ride around; some they snaked aside with lariats. An echoless silence held the blighted land; the roar of the river was loud in their ears. Partridge said, "Recollect where she might be?"

"I can only guess," Dan said, frowning. "Remember the rock that sticks out over the gorge like a thumb a couple of miles up? We made our jump from there. No telling how far downstream we went. But I'd guess she's somewhere along about here."

He dismounted and crawled to the lip of the gorge and looked down; he could see the racing river and the walls; he could see the ledges above the water line, but these ledges were bare, and his view was limited. He drew his gun and fired into the air three times, spacing out the shots. He listened then, hoping she might have heard and called out, but he supposed her voice wouldn't have lifted above the Purgatory's clamor. Still, he repeated his signal from time to time in the next hour as they moved slowly along the rim, peering over its edge intermittently.

Once Partridge held up his hand for silence. "Listen!" he said. "A shot! Somebody heard our signal and answered. To the west, I'd say, and higher up. At Digby's place."

"Clayton Allison," Dan guessed, and was not interested.

They continued their searching; they fired again, but there was no answering shot from the north. Dan watched the sun and saw it pass zenith and tasted despair; and then, upon his knees at the rim again, he looked down and saw her almost directly below him. He shouted, "April! April!" incoherently; she didn't hear him. He picked up a fist-sized rock and tossed it outward and saw it drop into the water near the ledge, dashing spray. She stood and raised her eyes then, searching for whoever had thrown the rock. He leaned far out and waved his arm frantically. She waved in return. He crawled back and hurried to his horse. "Barney," he cried, "give me a hand with the ropes! I've found her! Do you hear? I've found her!"

They'd brought every lariat they could find; they began knotting these lariats together, making one long rope out of them, and in the end of this Dan fashioned a loop. He found a place along the rim where the rock was smooth and there was no danger of the rope's sawing in half, and he flung the rope over and watched it snake far out and fall back against the near wall. The rope reached down to the ledge. Partridge fastened the end to his saddle horn, and Dan said, "I'm going down."

"No need for it," Partridge said. "If she can reach the rope, we can haul her up."

"I'm going down," Dan said again.

Wrapping his hands around the rope, he swung himself out over the rim. He braced his feet against the wall and let himself down slowly; there was little resiliency in him; he'd kept himself going too long and too hard. He put a brake upon his impatience, making the descent carefully; he tried not to look below. At last he was upon the ledge. April was to him instantly; she looked beaten; she looked done in. He took her in his arms and held her for a moment, stroking her hair. He said, "I was afraid I wouldn't find you in time."

She said, "I thought about trying to swim it, but I knew you'd come."

"We'll get you out of here fast," he said.

He dropped the loop over her head and shoulders, and drew it up snugly under her arms. He looked up; Partridge was leaning over the rim; Dan lifted his arm and signaled to Hourglass's foreman, and Partridge vanished, and shortly the slack went out of the rope and April began rising. Dan watched as best he could; he saw April reach the rim and Barney's hands help her. Shortly the rope came snaking down again, and he caught it and fastened the loop under his own arms and felt the tug of the cow pony at the other end of it and went spinning upward. Both Barney and April were waiting to help him; Partridge had snubbed the rope around a tree and the cow pony stood off at a distance, up the road, its feet braced.

Dan got to a stand and removed the rope and said, "Barney, this is April Allison."

Partridge fumbled off his hat and extended his hand, admiration in his grin. "I've seen you before, but never close up. You're a looker, even with your hair all stringy. Pleased to meet you."

Dan put his arm around her, steadying her. "We've food in the saddlebags. You must be famished."

She said, "More scared than starved. Time dragged down there." She shuddered. "I kept

251

worrying about you — and him."

"Fanshawe?"

She shook her head. "My father. I remembered the fire and wondered about him."

Dan said, "We'll go looking for him. Somebody signaled us a while ago."

She ate, and while she ate she talked; it was personal talk, and Partridge wandered off, displaying an intent interest in the rim and the skeleton woods beyond. She told Dan of her parting with her father and her hurrying to Fanshawe and the bargain she'd intended striking with Fanshawe. She told all this tonelessly; Dan squatted near her and told her of his last meeting with Fanshawe. She said, "He doesn't matter — he never did, really. He was someone who was kind to me because I was useful to him. I guess I was hungry for kindness. It's my dad I'm concerned about. Whatever he did, he must have had a reason for it. I've had a lot of time to think about that."

"We'll find him," Dan promised.

He helped her up into his own saddle when she was finished eating; he mounted behind her, and Partridge, who'd coiled up the long rope and hung it from his saddle horn, mounted too, and they rode onward up the road. Again they had to work around obstructions; they came to the jutting rock where April and Dan had made their jump. They looked, and April shuddered and said, "I don't think I could do it twice. Not even with you."

Dan dismounted and walked out upon the rock. "Here's your boots and my gun," he said, and picked up these articles and put them in his saddlebag.

Beyond the north line of Hourglass's holdings, they came upon a miracle; here the barrier of lodgepole pine still stood thick to the left of the trail; some vagary of the fire had spared this section of the hills, burning out the timber below it and to the west of it. They found the road Sam Digby had built in from the pass to his ranch; they threaded along this road; there was heat and utter silence and a sense of oppression in the air, but the fire hadn't been here. They came into the stump-mottled clearing where the sagging, peeled-pole fence enclosed the sprawling log house, and here they found Allison. He lay in his yard; he lay flat upon his back, his arms flung wide; and April saw him thus and moaned and came down from the horse and ran to him, falling on her knees beside him and cradling his head in her lap.

Dan and Partridge, dismounting, came forward, and Dan saw the blood upon Allison's shirt front. He knelt and felt for Allison's pulse and found a weak beating there. Dan said gently, "We'll get him into the house." He

253

saw that Allison's overalls were worn through at the knees, and he wondered how far the man had crawled.

Allison's six-shooter lay near his right hand. Partridge picked it up and jacked the used shells out of it and said, "Empty. That's why he didn't signal more than once."

They took hold of Allison and carried him to the house, April hurrying ahead and opening the door. She said, "Put him in my bedroom. Over here." Silence was in this house, silence and heat and faded carpeting and homemade furniture. She swept the curtain aside, and they brought Allison into the room with the clipping-covered walls and laid him upon the bed.

He opened his eyes then; he looked about him and said wearily, "I wondered if anybody would ever come."

Dan ripped apart the man's shirt and had a look at the wound, and Partridge, peering, said, "Reckon I should ride for Doc Church?" But there was no hope in Partridge's voice.

Allison said, "April —" and reached out his hand, and she took it. Allison looked at the two men and said, "Don't go. I want to talk while there's time."

Dan said gently, "I want to know who did this to you, but don't force yourself. Take it easy, Allison."

But he was thinking that Allison was as good as dead and that the man knew it. Allison had something he wanted off his chest. Maybe the greatest kindness would be to listen; Allison would be gone long before anybody could reach Ballardton.

Allison said, "I owe you the truth, Ballard. I owe it to you because I might have murdered you, if it hadn't been for her. You're a rich man, Ballard, if you only knew it. I've got to tell you about that — while I can."

Dan said, "The Purgatory?"

Allison tried to nod. "I'm an engineer. I've been making a hydrographic survey. Maybe you guessed as much when you saw the map out on the table the other day. I was afraid you had. I was afraid the whole scheme had gone smash. A dam on the Purgatory, down there in the gorge, would furnish electrical power and act as a reservoir to irrigate the entire range. My notes are here in the house, and any engineer can translate them for you. I prowled the country and found my site; I took soundings and drew a cross section of the river at the point of the dam site. I found the flow with a current meter. It's a natural, Ballard."

"What did you expect to gain?" Dan asked. "The Hourglass holds title to all of Purgatory Gorge."

"You were to be ruined and then bought out without your knowing what you were giving up," Allison said. "That was *his* scheme. With this drought it wasn't hard to stir up Old Man Cantrell to make trouble; that only took a word or two. *He* thought you'd sell out cheap, either before the fight or after. He's the one who guessed the river had possibilities for a dam site. He looked for an engineer who was down on his luck, one he could twist around his finger. He found me."

Bitterness brought the old cynicism into Allison's voice. "He found the right man for his crooked scheming. He arranged for me to take over this Digby place as a blind. All I was supposed to do was make this survey; he'd handle the rest."

Dan's voice turned cold. "Now I see it. Ransome Price. He offered to buy the Hourglass for some Eastern investors. No wonder you jumped me and hog-tied me when you found me looking at that map. And then you rode to tell him I was wise to his scheme."

"He said you had to die, Ballard. He sent me back here to kill you. I might have done it, but you'd got away. Then he sent me a note, saying it didn't matter. The Hourglass had defied Tomahawk and it meant war. He was sure you Ballards would be driven out. And he was sure you'd be willing to sell at any price, once the Cantrells had beaten you. That was Price's way, to work one ranch against the other and pick up the leavings."

Dan said, "The war's over, Allison. The Cantrells have lost. And so has Price."

Allison said, "I was willing to have a hand in a swindle, if that's what getting Purgatory meant. I didn't know I'd be expected to turn murderer before I was through. But here's the important thing, and I want you to know it. At the showdown I lined up with the Hourglass. I'm the man who set the woods afire."

"*You* started the fire!"

"My idea was to set a strip ablaze between the Tomahawk and the lower country. That way I hoped to keep the Cantrells from getting at the springs. But they saw the fire and knew they had to get through before it spread. They came riding, and I heard them coming. I made a stand against them, but I'm no man with a gun. They shot me down and rode on, leaving me. I managed to crawl back here. That's all of it."

Dan said aghast, "You stood up against the Cantrells *alone!*" He remembered Old Man Cantrell, his stiffening beard pointing at the sky; he remembered Cantrell with no regret.

Allison said, "You can thank her for anything I tried to do at the last." He looked

257

up at April. "She walked out on me. Before she did, she made me see myself as I really was."

He kept his eyes on her, and he said, "I want you to know this, my dear: I didn't want to do murder. That's why I had to get drunk first. I argued with Price; I told him there must be another way. He insisted that Ballard had to die. I refused to do the killing. Then he told me that he'd been standing near the jail the night Lew Fanshawe was snatched away. He told me he'd seen *you* ride away with Fanshawe. He claimed that Fanshawe was wanted for murder down in Utah and that it would be hard against you if the law knew you'd sprung Fanshawe from jail. He said he'd take the truth to the law if I didn't ride back here and take care of Ballard."

April came down to her knees beside the bed; she leaned close to her father and said, "Then it was partly for me? You were going to do it to protect me?"

He said, "I've been a poor father, but you counted for something with me, always. And when you told me how you felt about Ballard, I changed sides because of it. I wanted to do that for you; I wasn't sure you'd ever know about it. I thought you were gone forever."

He looked at Ballard and he said, "Take

very good care of her, my friend. Very good care."

He looked at April, and his eyes were glazed. He called a name; it wasn't her name; it was another name, and Dan remembered that photograph in the engineering book; he remembered that woman spoiled by a knowledge of her own beauty. Allison called that name and tried drawing April closer to him; he stiffened convulsively, and the candle of his life guttered out.

It took them all a full moment to realize he was gone, and then Dan thought, *He was going on sheer will at the last.* Allison had had to tell him the truth, and he had held on till the truth was out. Thinking this, Dan clawed off a sombrero he'd borrowed in the Hourglass camp and worn on this ride.

April came to a stand. She was dry-eyed, and he wondered if she understood, and he said gently, "We'll see that he's properly buried."

Still she didn't cry; the tears would come later. She said, an edge of hysteria to her voice, "The grave's already dug. The one he dug for you. Remember, I told you about that down by the gorge."

Dan said, "We'll leave you alone with him for a while."

He came through the outer room to the

porch; Partridge came with him and they stood silently together, Dan's jaw rigid with the run of his thoughts. Dan said then, "Will you stay here and attend to the burial, Barney? Me, I've got one more ride to make."

Partridge said, "Price?"

"Price!" Dan said.

"Don't tally him as too easy," Partridge said. "No man's ever seen a gun on him, but he carries one sometimes, and he's practiced a lot. Once I watched him from the rim of a coulee, months ago. He was puncturing some tin cans."

Dan said, "I wouldn't want him to be too easy."

He crossed the yard and climbed to his horse; he wheeled the horse about and sent it along the road leading back to Tomahawk Pass. He rode with his thoughts on the people he'd left behind him; he rode with his thoughts miles ahead on the man he would face before sundown. He remembered Gramp and the three things Gramp had told him he'd have to taste before he'd really have lived. He'd found a cause worth dying for — he'd wanted peace along the Purgatory or, failing that, the downfall of the Cantrells. He'd found love. He'd thought sometimes that he'd hated Fanshawe, but Fanshawe wasn't worthy of hate. He'd pitted himself against the Cantrells, but even that had been impersonal. But now there was Price. And now there was hate. Thus had he found the last of the three.

19

Crossfire

He hit Hourglass in late afternoon, riding hard. He tarried here only long enough to change horses. Wayne and the wounded had not yet come back from town; the chuck wagon stood in the yard, and some of the men were in the bunkhouse. They had done a burying job at Ballard Springs — Dan had seen the mounds as he'd come past — but they'd brought Pete back to the home ranch; they had Pete laid out in the bunkhouse with a blanket over him, and they would do a proper job for him later. Dan asked about Gramp. Gramp was in his room and had been sleeping the last time anybody had looked in on him. Gramp could rest; his work was done.

A fresh horse under him, Dan humped up over the caprock rim and lined out for town. He could see the buildings far south across the flats; he could see the high lift of the church spire, and he remembered the wedding that had been postponed. He thought of Cynthia and recalled her saying, "Not long ago I said that you seemed to attract violence. Now I know that you go out looking for it." He reflected grimly that she ought to see him now!

This side of the prairie-dog village, he met Wayne and the three wounded Hourglass men who had gone into Ballardton with Wayne. Dan had watched the group draw closer to him; he had recognized them and thus rode toward them with no fear. They all drew rein, and Dan saw that Wayne was keeping one foot out of stirrup, holding it stiff, and Dan said, "What did Doc Church think?"

"He claims we'll all live," Wayne said, and smiled. His eyes searched Dan's. "You found her, kid?"

"She's up at Digby's place. Barney's with her. Clayton Allison is dead, Wayne. Before he died, he talked. I'm on my way to hunt down Ransome Price. He's the one who was behind all the trouble on this range. Barney will tell you the whole of it."

Wayne eyed him thoughtfully. "I'll send the boys on to the ranch, Dan. You're out to make a fight. I'll be at your back when you do."

Dan thought, *He's found himself today, and he'll never run from trouble again,* and a surging pride was in him. He reined closer and lifted a hand to Wayne's shoulder, gripping it hard. He said, "This is a one-man job, Wayne, and I'm the Ballard with a whole skin today. Better go on to the ranch. There won't be much to this."

But he was remembering what Barney Par-

263

tridge had told him about Ransome Price's secret skill with a gun.

Wayne said, "I guess I wouldn't be much real help at that. I'm going to have to be using Gramp's cane for a week. But at least the odds won't be stacked against you in town. Abe Potter told me that the Cantrell boys and their help rode through around noon. After the fight at the springs, they must have made a wide scale through the foothills and lined out for the town. They stopped only long enough to buy grub for their saddlebags, then headed on south."

Dan said, "I'll be getting along."

Wayne said, "Good luck, kid," and it was the way he said it that made them brothers again.

Dan jogged his mount and skirted the group, giving a wave to the men who'd been wounded today for Hourglass. Not looking back, he rode onward. He saw the shadows of the sage clumps grow long and cool and purple; he saw the day die, and he came to Ballardton in the last light and rode along the grayed street and tied up his horse before the Rialto and went jingling his spurs along the boardwalk on the far side of the street, until he came to Ransome Price's office.

The little building was locked, but there was no *Back Soon* sign upon the door. Frowning,

Dan turned away; he saw the portly figure of Abe Potter coming along. He greeted Potter, and the town marshal sighed and said, "A little excitement out your way today, I hear tell."

Dan said, "Work for you, Abe?"

"I'll send a report to the sheriff. I talked to Wayne this afternoon. It's just routine. The Tomahawk got what it asked for. I see that smoke's still standing over the hills. I reckon the fire wiped out Cantrell's spread. What do you suppose started it?"

Dan shrugged. "We'll never know," he said, and reflected that this was the second time he'd lied to the law for the sake of an Allison.

"I wish it would rain," Potter said.

"Seen Ransome Price?"

Potter thumbed back his sombrero and thought carefully. "Not lately," he said. "Now wait a minute. He was in Ching Li's. Having a mighty early supper, I thought."

Dan said, "Thanks," and went on down the street; he passed Lily Greer's millinery shop; he came to the restaurant and opened its screen door. The smell of food smote him; only then did he remember that he was very hungry. He looked at the row of stools along the counter; he looked at the tables. Quite a few men were here at this hour; Price was not one of them. He said, "Anybody seen Ransome Price?"

They had stared at him as he stood framed in the doorway; he'd forgotten about his battered face, his singed and shapeless clothes. But their stares held not surprise but respect, a new evaluating of him, and he guessed that the story of Hourglass's fight had gone the rounds. A man who smelled strong of horses said, "You'll find him down at my livery stable. He keeps his horse there, and he came in just as I was going out to eat. Better hurry. He's taking himself a trip; he wanted me to saddle up for him, but I didn't have time."

Dan said, "I'm obliged."

He about-faced and headed up the boardwalk; he came past the Palace and there were no Tomahawk horses at the hitchrail, and it seemed odd to think there would never again be Tomahawk horses there. He went on; he remembered that the last time he'd walked this way had been when he'd gone toward the jail building in the hope of saving Lew Fanshawe from a lynch mob. That had been just a few nights ago; that had been an eternity ago. Soon he was beyond the hub of the town's activity, and here was the feed and livery stable. Before this very door he'd found Price lounging that night, lounging and smoking a cigar and making talk of what fools men were.

Now the door was wide open, and he paused before it and lifted his gun from leather and let it drop back into the holster. He took a scraping step and framed himself in the doorway; he stepped into a veil of quietness lighted by a single lantern set upon an upturned box. Back yonder were stalls and darkness and the slow munching of horses, the restless stomping of horses, these things and a movement made by a man.

Dan said softly, "Price? Ransome Price?"

He saw the suitcase then; it was set upon the floor near one of the rear stalls; it hadn't yet been tied to a saddle. This wasn't to have been a short trip to talk over a land deal with some drought-ridden rancher. Price intended shaking the dust of the Purgatory from his boots. Price moved into the cone of light cast by the lantern; he stood there with his sensuous face drawn tight by some inward strain, his eyes expressionless. He said, "Well, Ballard?"

Dan said, "Leaving us?"

"Some business in Helena," Price said. "There's no train for two days and stage connections are poor."

Dan said, "You might do business here. It's lucky I caught you in time. You came to Wayne with a proposition, Price. I'd like to talk about that. I'd like to know if you still

267

want to buy the Hourglass."

Price sucked in a hard breath. "You don't mean it!"

Dan said, "You've heard. You know we beat the Cantrells today. You know we don't need a way out."

"That's it," Price said.

Suddenly Dan was through with this kind of talking; he had thought to play cat-and-mouse with this man. He had relished the thought, but now there was in him no desire but to have this over and done with. A harshness crept into his voice, and he said, "No, the Hourglass isn't for sale. We'll hold on to it and find some Eastern investors who'll be willing to put a dam on the Purgatory on a shares basis. The same kind of deal you had tied up when you set out to lay your hands on the Hourglass. It's a natural; that river. Clayton Allison said so."

In a flat voice Price said, "So you know!"

"Everything," Dan said. "You were afraid I did. That's why you're running out. You showed your cards when you rode to Ballard Springs last night; you thought the Tomahawk would put us under it and it wouldn't matter. But the Ballards have won; the Ballards are kingpins on this range now and forever, and you lined yourself against us. That means you're through here. You couldn't do much

268

business on this range now — not even honest business. So you're tucking your tail between your legs and running."

Price said, "Is that all?"

The hate grew in Dan and consumed him, and he remembered Gramp saying, "Did you ever hate a man so much that nothing would satisfy you but to lay your bare hands on him?"

He said, "Only this, Price. The Cantrells wanted something that wasn't theirs, but they were willing to run a risk to get it. I can respect them for that. But you were the kind who played safe. You prodded a range war into starting; you were willing to set neighbor against neighbor and see the whole range running red just because it would give you your opportunity. You were willing to climb over a pile of dead men and not give a damn about them. I couldn't hate the Cantrells. But I want you to know that I hate you. And I want you to know why."

Price said savagely, "To hell with you, Ballard!" and raised his hand toward the shoulder holster he wore. Dan saw that gesture; he'd been waiting for it, and his hand jerked toward his own gun, a quick, stabbing movement, and he was remembering Gramp and the badgers again. The bullet came; it breathed hotly past Dan's face, but it didn't come from Price's gun. A shadowy stall to

Dan's left had blossomed flame; a man was in there and triggering, and even before Price shouted, *"Fanshawe!"* Dan knew and understood.

There were the two of them, and they had him in a crossfire, and with the knowledge of this he went down to the spongy dirt of the runway and rolled, firing as he rolled. The lantern blinked with the concussion, wavering and almost going out. Price's gun was speaking; the bullets lifted the dirt and flung it into Dan's face, but in Dan was a thought which he held to with cool calculation. *One at a time!* He blazed in the direction of that stall to the left; he fired at the flame of Fanshawe's gun; and Fanshawe came lurching out into the light, the gun still in his hand, the gun a dead weight in his hand. Fanshawe fell heavily, dropping across Dan's legs, and Fanshawe was dead when he fell.

Now Dan turned his gun, seeking out Price and knowing a frantic desperation because the weight of Fanshawe pinned him to the floor and kept him from rolling. Horses were pitching in the stalls; the one Price had saddled kicked out, the hoofs grazing Price who took a staggering sideward step; and that gave Dan his moment. Price fired again; the bullet tugged at Dan's shirt; but Dan put a cool precision to his shooting now; he got Price in the sight and triggered and saw Price's heavy gold watch chain leap, and Price stepped backward as though he were impaled. Price looked at him; Price's eyes were cold and fathomless, and then the intelligence was gone out of them. Price's knees gave beneath him and he went down and lay in a tumbled heap like a pile of discarded clothes.

Dan got to his feet and stood unsteadily for a moment; the smell of burned powder was heavy in here; he thought he heard the thud of boots along the boardwalk. That would be men drawn by the sounds of gunfire. He crossed over and looked down at Price, and Price was dead. He remembered himself saying to Gramp, "When I leave a dead man behind me, I want to feel in my bones that he deserved to die." He looked at Price, and there was no respect in him.

He went to where Fanshawe lay. Fanshawe's lips were skinned back in a grimace, showing those teeth so startlingly white and perfect. This grimace Fanshawe would carry with him through eternity. Dan thought, "I should have known," and found that he'd said it aloud. Fanshawe had heard that a war was shaping along the Purgatory, and he'd come to hire himself out to the Hourglass, but Barney had sent him packing. So he'd found someone else to buy his guns. And with this knowledge, Dan understood many things.

He knew now why Ransome Price had stood in this livery stable's doorway, listening to the sounds of building fury the night Fanshawe's life had been in jeopardy, listening and pretending an indifference to Fanshawe's fate. He knew why Price had held his tongue about the truth of Fanshawe's escape. And he knew why Fanshawe had tried from the first to pick a fight with him; Fanshawe had had a personal hate, but Fanshawe had also wanted Dan dead because Price had wanted him dead. Wayne, standing alone, was to have been easier to handle.

Fanshawe's horse was here in the livery stable, impounded by Abe Potter after Fanshawe's arrest the day of the wedding. Fanshawe was to have ridden out with Price, and Fanshawe had faded into the shadows at the sound of Dan beyond the doorway when Dan had first come here tonight, for Fanshawe was a wanted man. There was another horse saddled, too. Dan looked at it, seeing the gentleness of the beast, seeing the side-saddle.

He walked to the doorway and through it. He felt the night air against him and it was good; the day's heat was gone, the day's violence was done. A group of men was coming on the run, and one of them was Abe Potter.

272

Potter saw Dan and came to a heavy stop and said, "What is it?"

"Two dead men inside," Dan said. "You'll find guns in their hands. That makes it a fair fight. If you look in the alleys, I think you'll find a saddler with Sam Digby's old brand; one of the fellows inside wanted to ride out on his own horse. You can tack this onto that report you're sending the sheriff. It's all of the same cloth."

Potter dragged his sleeve across his forehead. He said wearily, "Is there no end to it?"

Dan said, "Don't worry. It's all finished now. All that the law will have anything to do with anyway."

20

The Trail Home

When he got up the street as far as the Rialto, he climbed upon his waiting horse and jerked at the tie-rope, then sat his saddle indecisively for a long moment, knowing the one thing that had yet to be done and hating the thought of it. He got the horse into motion, letting it take a slow walk, and kneed it along the street until he was beyond the busier part of town and the buildings thinned out and the better residences stood neatly spaced apart.

He came to the cottage of Doc Church and dismounted in the shadow of the giant cottonwood, looping the reins over the picket fence. He walked slowly to the porch and rapped upon the door; the waiting wasn't long; the door opened and Doc Church stood there. He looked and saw Dan, and surprise made Church a little foolish for a moment. He said, "Come in. Come in," but there wasn't a great deal of enthusiasm to it.

Dan said, "Cynthia?" and then, peering past Church, he saw her.

She sat here in the parlor, and she was part of its studied elegance; she fitted well against this background of plush furniture and

Battenberg lace curtains and red drapes held by white, tasseled cords. She wore that long, trailing dress of rustling stuff she'd worn the day he'd come home, but over it was a linen duster, and her hat and veil were in place, and on the floor near her feet a suitcase rested. She had looked up eagerly as the door had opened; her eyes were alive for a moment, and then the expectancy that made them alive was gone out of her.

Dan said, "You thought I was Price."

It wasn't a question and it called for no answer. Doc Church stood, a man awkward and embarrassed, and Dan said, "It's all right, Doc. We talked it out under the cottonwood a few nights ago, and there were no strings on her. But Price won't be coming. He's dead."

He hadn't meant to give it to her quite that way; he saw her reel, but she didn't faint. Dan said, "I meant to come here tonight anyway, to ask you to release me from whatever was left of a promise between us. I guess that was already taken care of."

Cynthia stared at him and her voice was empty. "He came to me this afternoon and asked me to marry him. We were to be married in Helena; he had to leave quickly. Some business, he said." Her voice broke, and grief had its way with her. "Dan! Dan!" she cried.

"Why did you do it?"

"Not because of you," he said gently. He remembered Fanshawe; he wondered if Price had meant that Fanshawe was to ride away with them, too; he wondered if Fanshawe was to have fitted into some other scheme on some other range. "Perhaps I did you a favor," he said. "There may be a day when you'll believe that."

He turned toward the door; there was no more to be said. Cynthia looked at him; she had herself in hand again, and she said, "This is good-bye between you and me, Dan?" In the glow of a lamp her face stood etched in all its perfection; there was hope in her eyes and a shrewd calculation. Odd, Dan thought, that he should remember at this moment the flowers she'd carried the day of the postponed wedding — the artificial flowers — and that he should remember, too, the townsman he'd once struck because the fellow had intimated that a girl was no fool who married a half-interest in the Hourglass. But he only said, "Whenever you looked at me alive, you'd remember him dead. Yes, it's good-bye, Cynthia."

He stepped out through the door and Doc Church followed after him. He got to the horse and stood with one hand upon the horn, and Church's face was lost in the shadow of the cottonwood. Church said, "I'm not asking how it happened, Daniel. I'll hear soon enough, I suppose. I never felt sure of him. I want you to know that."

Dan said gently, "On the outside he looked like her kind of man. I can understand that. And his prospects were good. I hold no grudge. She's ready for traveling. Send her away for a while, Doc. That's what she needs."

"Perhaps," Church said. "She has an aunt in Indiana."

Dan stepped up into saddle. Cynthia would never come back, he knew. This land had been too much for her, and she'd find her kind of people and her way of living somewhere else, and she'd never come back. He thought of Price and he wondered then if Cynthia was another reason why Lew Fanshawe's gun had been hired against him; Dan's wedding might have come off, if it hadn't been for Fanshawe. Had Price really loved her? Was that why he'd been going to take her with him on the ride out, or was it a shred of triumph he'd hope to take, the woman who was supposed to belong to a Ballard? Dan turned this over in his mind and found that it didn't matter.

He lifted his hand in salute to Doc Church and went riding back up the street.

The aftermath of released tension left him

almost sick; he saw the Rialto again and wondered if he should buy himself a drink, but he knew he didn't want a drink. He took the road north, building a cigarette as he rode along, and he got some comfort from the tobacco. He looked ahead to the lifting hills; their high crests were blotted out by smoke. He rode numbly, almost too tired to think, and it came to him then, the full realization. He was free! Free of everything. Free of violence and bloodshed and worry, free of his promise to Cynthia, free to take up the dreams that were left off when he'd come home and found this mess. It was a good thought, and he carried it with him across the miles to the Hourglass.

Light showed in the ranch house when he came down off the caprock rim, and there was activity in the yard, even at this late hour. The crew had a sleeplessness in them and he could understand that, remembering how he'd wanted a drink and yet not wanted it. He gave his horse to the first man who shaped up, and he climbed the gallery then and stepped into the big room. Wayne was here, seated in a chair with his hurt leg propped stiffly before him, and Barney Partridge was here, too, seated across from Wayne. Dan looked at Hourglass's foreman and said, "April?"

"Up at Digby's place," Partridge said. "We

got her dad buried and she began taking it hard when the dirt fell. She wanted to be alone, so I left her. There's nothing in those hills that could do her harm now."

Wayne said, "Barney's told me all about Price and Allison and the hydrographic survey. That explained a lot of things. Now I know why you had to make your ride tonight."

"Price is dead," Dan said. "So is Fanshawe. He was Price's man. Either Allison didn't know that, or he didn't have time to tell me."

Wayne said, "You looked worked-over. You'll be anxious to bed down."

Dan said, "We can do the rest of the talking in the morning."

He climbed the stairs; that one step creaked beneath him. He came along the hall and saw that Gramp's door was partially open, and a faint glow of light fell out into the hall. He stepped into the doorway; Gramp was in bed, propped up against pillows but not sleeping; a lamp burned dimly on a stand beside the bed. Dan crossed to the bed and sat upon the edge of it and said, "How are you feeling, Gramp?"

"How would I be feeling after a day like today?" Gramp said testily. "I had no business leaving this room. You know that."

Dan said, "You'll be out and around soon.

We'll need you. We've got a ranch to run."

Gramp frowned. "Are you and Wayne going to lean on me till the day I die? What's the matter with the pair of you running the ranch and letting me have a little rest for a change? Wayne's supposed to know the range, and you're supposed to be educated. What the hell good was all that book-learning if this place can't produce a better breed of cattle? Damn it, Daniel, the pair of you make me tired!"

Dan came to a stand; unconsciously he raised his hand to his shoulder where Gramp's cane had struck him, and the pain was gone. He smiled down at Gramp and said, "Good night, you old son of a gun!"

He went to his own room and stripped off his singed clothing and lay naked upon the bed without getting under the covers. The air was stifling; the heat pressed down upon him like a hard hand. He lay sleepless; he saw the outline of that trunkful of books in the corner. He'd have to get them unpacked. That was one of the first things he'd have to do. He dozed and awoke and dozed again; a great deal of the tension ran out of him; he soaked up rest.

While it was still dark he surrendered to an urge that had persisted in gnawing at the edge of his consciousness, keeping him from full sleep. He came off the bed and rustled up fresh clothing and donned it; and he crept carefully down the stairs, not wishing to disturb Wayne or Gramp. The bunkhouse was dark when he crossed the yard. He saddled a horse and stepped up into saddle and lined out to the north, riding easily.

He passed Ballard Springs just at dawn; he saw the graves the Hourglass men had dug; he looked at the wire-enclosed water and the cattle which stood sluggishly before the wire. The whole range had worried about this spring, he reflected; Cantrell had wanted it so much that he'd died wanting it. And all the while the real worth of the Hourglass had been up there in that useless river, and none of them had seen it!

Not so very long thereafter he was toiling upward and at last he was into that desolate land of dead ash and blackened timber and he reined short upon the jutting rock and listened to the rumble of the Purgatory below. He tried to picture the dam that would be built; it would mean power, and stored-up water; they'd never have to worry about another drought.

He rode on; the light was upon the land, but it was a dismal light, gray and uncertain, and the air held that same oppression he had felt in his bedroom. He turned off onto the road Sam Digby had built; he came at last into the stump-mottled clearing before the log house. He left the horse standing in the yard and stepped to the porch and pushed at the door; there was only silence, silence and an air of desertion; and he was panicked with the thought that she might be gone from here, gone from his life. He called her name and an answer came to him, low and incoherent and sounding like a sob. He crossed to the curtain at her bedroom door and thrust it aside. She lay face down upon the bed, fully clothed and crying. He sat down beside her, saying nothing for a while, and then he laid his hand upon her shoulder.

He said, "He was just a man who took the wrong turn of the trail somewhere. When he found where he was headed, he turned back. Always remember that a lot of men wouldn't have done that."

Her crying ceased; he lifted her, taking her into his arms; he looked down into her face and saw what grief had done to it. He said, "I've come to take you home."

"Home?"

He said, "I love you. I didn't dare say that before, not even to myself, because I was half promised to someone else. That's not so now." He remembered Gramp saying, "You haven't lived, Dan. You haven't known what it is to want a woman the minute you lay eyes on her, and to know that nothing could be more important than marrying her — pronto." But he *had* known. He'd known that night in the jail corridor when he'd found her freeing Fanshawe, but he'd turned his face from the truth. Now he could understand why he'd lied to Abe Potter and all those others in Doc Church's office when they'd asked him about that jail delivery.

She stirred in his arms, her own kind of pride showing in her eyes, and he saw that she was close to crying again, but the astonishing thing was that she was trying to break free of him. She said, "I don't want your pity! I heard my father ask a promise of you in this very room. You don't have to spend the rest of your life keeping it."

He got her by the shoulders and shook her angrily. "You little fool!" he said. "Do you suppose I want you for anybody's sake but your own? I've told you that I love you. There's only one thing I want to hear out of you. Say it, April. Say it!"

But still her pride was in her, tinged now by awe and unbelief and a timorous grasping at a miracle. "I saw *her* once," she said. "The day of the wedding. She's a grand lady, the kind you'd want for mistress of the Hourglass. I couldn't fill her shoes, Dan."

He laughed then, glorying in her self-pride,

glorying in her humbleness, and, remembering the shallow soul of Cynthia and the courage of this girl beside him, he groped for words to tell her how it was with him, and, failing to find the words, he drew her close again. "Once before, we made a jump together," he said. "Believe me, we won't be taking a chance this time. Say it, April!"

"I love you," she said, and buried her face against his shoulder. "I did from the first. Dad knew that. I told him so last night. Oh, Dan, are you very sure you want me?"

He made his reply in his own way, and after that she said nothing; she sighed. He held her for a long time, stroking her hair and kissing her gently.

Suddenly she tore free from him again and sat bolt upright and said, "Listen! Do you hear it? On the roof! *Rain!*"

It reached into his consciousness then, that light patter as of fairy fingers, that steady beating that grew louder and louder. He remembered the light that had been no real light; he remembered the heaviness in the air. He hadn't seen clouds around the peaks; he couldn't have seen them because of the pall of smoke. He listened to the miracle of rain on the roof, and then both of them were seized with the same urge, and they went running through the house and out into the yard and watched the ground hiss to the touch of rain. Dan stood with his face upturned and let the rain fall upon it, and at first he was deliriously happy, and then he grew angry.

He thought, *Why couldn't this have come a week ago?* And he thought how different everything might have been for himself and Wayne and Cynthia and the Cantrells and Ransome Price and Fanshawe. He thought of the hate that might have been washed away by this, but he knew then that all the things that had happened were bound to have happened, the drought had only hurried them. The drought had appraised them and some had been found wanting. And now the drought was through, gone down to sizzling defeat; and he forgave the drought.

He said, "We'd better be starting. From the looks of this, it's going to keep up all day."

"It will put out the forest fire," she said.

They went back into the house and he found a slicker that had belonged to Sam Digby. He wrapped it around her and laughed at the sight of her in it. She picked a roll of paper from the table. She said, "The topographical map and Dad's notes," and she tucked the bundle under her slicker.

Outside, he mounted and reached down for her and got her into his arms. Her face was very close to his, and he kissed her.

She said, "Dan, I'm scared! Your folks —"

He said, "You saw the look on Barney Partridge's face when he met you yesterday. That's how it will be with my brother Wayne when he shakes hands. But there's another that I'm most anxious to take you to. He's an old man who met you once before, long, long ago, in a Comanche camp on the Sante Fe trail."

She didn't understand what he was talking about; he knew that. But the fear was gone from her face. She had placed herself in his hands; she had placed her future in his hands. He would see that she was never sorry. He drew her closer to him and jogged the horse into motion and put his back to Digby's place and went riding through the dripping woods, through the slanting rain.

The employees of THORNDIKE PRESS hope you have enjoyed this Large Print book. All our Large Print titles are designed for easy reading, and all our books are made to last. Other Thorndike Large Print books are available at your library, through selected bookstores, or directly from us. For more information about current and upcoming titles, please call or mail your name and address to:

THORNDIKE PRESS
PO Box 159
Thorndike, Maine 04986
800/223-6121
207/948-2962